Cambridge Elements

Elements in Crime Narratives
edited by
Margot Douai'
Emerson Colleg
Catherine Nicke
Emory College of Arts ar
Henry Sutto
University of East A

WRITING THE DETECTIVES

Character and the Series Form

Elspeth Latimer
University of East Anglia

CAMBRIDGE
UNIVERSITY PRESS

Shaftesbury Road, Cambridge CB2 8EA, United Kingdom

One Liberty Plaza, 20th Floor, New York, NY 10006, USA

477 Williamstown Road, Port Melbourne, VIC 3207, Australia

314–321, 3rd Floor, Plot 3, Splendor Forum, Jasola District Centre, New Delhi – 110025, India

103 Penang Road, #05–06/07, Visioncrest Commercial, Singapore 238467

Cambridge University Press is part of Cambridge University Press & Assessment, a department of the University of Cambridge.

We share the University's mission to contribute to society through the pursuit of education, learning and research at the highest international levels of excellence.

www.cambridge.org
Information on this title: www.cambridge.org/9781009502467
DOI: 10.1017/9781009502412

© Elspeth Latimer 2025

This publication is in copyright. Subject to statutory exception and to the provisions of relevant collective licensing agreements, no reproduction of any part may take place without the written permission of Cambridge University Press & Assessment.

When citing this work, please include a reference to the DOI 10.1017/9781009502412

First published 2025

A catalogue record for this publication is available from the British Library

ISBN 978-1-009-50246-7 Hardback
ISBN 978-1-009-50244-3 Paperback
ISSN 2755-1873 (online)
ISSN 2755-1865 (print)

Cambridge University Press & Assessment has no responsibility for the persistence or accuracy of URLs for external or third-party internet websites referred to in this publication and does not guarantee that any content on such websites is, or will remain, accurate or appropriate.

For EU product safety concerns, contact us at Calle de José Abascal, 56, 1°, 28003 Madrid, Spain, or email eugpsr@cambridge.org

Writing the Detectives

Character and the Series Form

Elements in Crime Narratives

DOI: 10.1017/9781009502412
First published online: August 2025

Elspeth Latimer
University of East Anglia

Author for correspondence: Elspeth Latimer,
E.Latimer@uea.ac.uk

Abstract: Crime fiction first emerged in the Victorian era and its series form continues to dominate the genre. Despite the prevalence of crime series, very little research has been done on how character is conceived. The Element's focus is contemporary, from the 1970s onward, and it determines the literary theory and conventions behind writing the detectives in these modern meganarratives. Exemplary series and a range of subgenres are analysed, thriller to cosy crime, professional investigator to amateur sleuth, embracing diversity and different gender identities. Previous examinations have tended to interpret the detective figure as either mythic or realist, but the author argues that both modes are combined in the contemporary crime series, generating a mythorealist protagonist. This creative-critical Element celebrates the vibrancy of the form and its capacity to investigate the human condition. It also considers future trends and concludes with the author's own guide to writing a crime fiction series.

Keywords: contemporary crime fiction, series, detective, amateur sleuth, protagonist, character, meganarrative, crime writing

© Elspeth Latimer 2025

ISBNs: 9781009502467 (HB), 9781009502443 (PB), 9781009502412 (OC)
ISSNs: 2755-1873 (online), 2755-1865 (print)

Contents

1 Introduction   1

2 Creating and Curating Character   5

3 Mythorealism   18

4 Iconically Masculine?   29

5 Character in Extremis   40

6 'An Underappreciated Revolution in Storytelling'   49

7 Writing a Crime Fiction Series   57

References   66

1 Introduction

Crime fiction first emerged in the Victorian era and its series form has proved popular ever since, with the latest debuts often attracting a global readership. Each crime series has unique qualities, but underlying the apparent differences there are techniques that authors apply, adapt, and subvert when creating their protagonist. In literature studies, very little research has been done to establish how these characters are conceived. My focus is contemporary, from the 1970s onward, and I determine the literary theory and conventions behind writing the detectives. A range of subgenres is considered, from thriller to cosy crime, from professional investigator to amateur sleuth, embracing diversity, and different gender identities. Previous examinations have tended to interpret the detective figure as either mythic or realist, but I argue that both modes are combined in the contemporary crime fiction series. This generates a mythorealist protagonist, who leads a recognisably everyday existence while retaining the features of mythic archetypes.

Through analyses of exemplary series along with author interviews, I demonstrate that mythorealism is fundamental to our creative-critical understanding of the detective figure. Contemporary crime series can span millions of words as well as decades of time, and author Laurie King points to the benefits of duration: 'Because I write about people and how they move and change, 300 pages isn't enough to complete a good, strong character. A series is a sort of mega-fiction: 3000 pages, divided into 10 episodes' (quoted in Jones & Walton, 1999: 56–7). To highlight the scale of this literary form I apply the term meganarrative, where I reconceive the crime series as a single text, allowing me to expose the structures that underpin it (Latimer, 2020: 7). As will become apparent, it is a text that is open-ended, creating opportunities for a protagonist to continue without termination. A meganarrative is also ideally suited to conveying a metanarrative or overarching message: a series author often has certain themes, explored in successive novels. But this study is about form rather than content, and my thesis is the primacy of character.

There is extensive scholarship on character theory in literary fiction, usually directed at one-off figures in standalone novels. Ideas relevant to the series form can, however, be found in research on transtextual fiction. These are narratives where an author borrows a secondary character from a canonical work, making them the protagonist of their own novel: for example, Jean Rhys's *Wide Sargasso Sea* conceived as a prequel to Charlotte Brontë's *Jane Eyre*. In Rosen's study of transtextual fiction, he suggests 'when contemporary authors become fascinated with a minor figure they dramatically extend, and physically enact with the production of a new fiction, a process of supplementation' (2016: 157–8).

Supplementation of character is intrinsic to the series form, and Ian Rankin, author of the Inspector Rebus series, refers to this when he shares his experiences of creating a long-running character: 'I've had millions of words I've been able to write about Rebus's life, and every time I write a little bit more about him, I find out a little bit more about the inside of his head' (2016). The idea of character construction as a process of infilling and augmentation has been examined by Margolin, and although not directed at series fiction, his views indicate how character manifests in these meganarratives:

> textually created characters are radically incomplete as regards the number and nature of the properties ascribed to them. Generally, which (kinds of) properties are specified or not and how many are a function of the text's length and of the author's artistic method ... [Characters] are technically person-kinds who can be filled in (specified, concretized) in various ways and to different degrees (2007: 68).

This suggests that an author creates a person-kind by giving them properties, such as physical description, actions, thoughts, dialogue, and a longer text allows more properties to be specified, enabling a reader to imagine a character that is potentially more 'complete' or concretised. Rankin has made a human-like figure, and each novel in the series becomes a way of expanding his and the reader's perception of Rebus.

The impetus to keep adding to a character is noted by Danielsson, a key scholar on crime series. She was first to conduct detailed research on the contemporary form and is crucial in identifying the type of protagonist that now dominates the genre: 'the former cardboard figure has ... turned into a dynamic character, with a private life and personal problems' (2003: 1). Novels from earlier series, such as Agatha Christie's Miss Marple or Raymond Chandler's Philip Marlowe, can be read in any order; they are self-contained and do not rely on prior knowledge from other novels in the same series. Nor do these figures tend to have an evolved personal life or much sense of an ongoing existence, hence Danielsson's critique of them as 'cardboard'. However, in the 1970s this static conception of character changes, when authors come to the genre with different ideas on how to create a series protagonist. There is a move toward greater continuity and complexity, resulting in new conventions that are still influencing those writing today:

> A contemporary detective series typically has a recurring protagonist who is depicted as existing in a world which goes on between books, a world in which actions in book number one have an effect in books number two and three. There are numerous references to events that have taken place in and between earlier installments, both regarding earlier 'cases' and regarding developments in the protagonist's personal life, such as love stories, illnesses, family and other relationships (Danielsson, 2002: 13–14).

This definition refers to 'detective series' but I categorise them as 'crime fiction series'. Here I follow Anderson, Miranda and Pezzotti, in their anthology on the crime series, who propose '"crime fiction" should be understood as a general term covering a wide range of subgenres (for example whodunits, thrillers, police procedurals, detective novels, noir and the like)' (2015: 7, citing Knight and Priestman). My choice of the term 'crime fiction series' also acknowledges that the protagonist investigating the crime is not necessarily a traditional detective; they could be a lawyer, a journalist, an art dealer, or a jockey, rather than a police inspector or private investigator.

Each novel in a contemporary crime series typically involves the detective figure being on a quest to solve a 'case'. This tends to be a murder or suspicious death, and Danielsson notes that in addition to the investigation, there are long story arcs about the personal life of the protagonist, 'who is depicted as existing in a world which goes on between books'. This she attributes to the influence of the *roman-fleuve* (2002: 141), a literary form exemplified by Anthony Powell's twelve-volume sequence *A Dance to the Music of Time*, with its cast of recurring characters. Danielsson also suggests crime series have become more like the serials on TV and radio, where each episode is an increment of a larger story. The feature that crime authors adopt from these other genres is, she states, 'a focus on the ongoing life of the protagonist' (2002: 141). Jones and Walton point to publishing trends as a contributory factor: 'Works in a series are routinely marketed by appealing to the reader's investment in a character and continuing interest in his or her life story' (1999: 152).

The life-story arc is the most significant change to the crime fiction series since it first emerged in the 1840s. Credit for that change belongs, I argue, to innovative female authors, often with a feminist politics, writing in the latter decades of the twentieth century. As Section 4 will demonstrate, by situating their detective figure within a network of friends and familial relationships, and carrying that group forward from novel to novel, this led to a biographic impulse that has transformed the genre. There is still a readership for the more discrete series of the Victorian or Golden Age or Hardboiled eras, where the texts are not intended to construct a sequence. However, for readers seeking the continuity of an unfolding chronology, they can turn to contemporary series, 'contemporary' defining when the novels are written rather than when they are set. For example, Sujata Massey's Perveen Mistry series is set in 1920s India but published in 2018, and the author follows current practice by creating an ongoing 'life' for her protagonist. It is also worth restating that my study is confined to series with a detective figure. There is an alternative class of series with a criminal as the lead character, where the plot centres on the protagonist perpetrating crimes while evading capture: for example, Patricia Highsmith's Tom Ripley series or

Elmore Leonard's Chili Palmer novels. However, criminal-protagonist fictions have their own conventions, distinct from those examined here.

The investigative figure in contemporary series usually belongs to one of these categories: *professional detective* employed to solve a murder, either in the police service or a private investigator; what I term a *semi-professional detective* who solves a murder using the transferrable skills from their role as lawyer, forensic pathologist, forensic psychologist, investigative journalist, and other comparable occupations; *amateur detective*, also known as amateur sleuth, who stumbles on a murder and feels compelled to solve it, often for personal reasons, and who has a day job unrelated to crime, such as chef, archaeologist, florist, librarian, artist, and so on. The protagonist may be a composite figure, for instance Lee Child's Jack Reacher discussed in Section 2, who combines aspects of amateur/professional detective. When considering different series from across the genre, it is apparent that the detective figure sometimes commits criminal acts (again exemplified by Reacher, who routinely kills his adversaries) but their primary role is to pursue an investigation and solve the murder or major crime(s) that catalyses the plot.

There are no recent studies that accurately define how the detective figure, professional, semi-professional, amateur, is created and maintained in contemporary crime fiction series; insufficient research has been done on the underlying conventions. Danielsson and Jones and Walton, working in the late 1990s and early 2000s, have increased our understanding, but I contend that their interpretations are incomplete. Danielsson proposes that the 'detective series ... has developed from a chronicle of murder cases to a life story in installments' (2003: 1), reflecting Jones and Walton's position that this 'biographical impetus remains central for detective fiction' (1999: 152). However, by focusing on the protagonist's life story, these critics have not addressed the continuing importance of the 'detection' within such fictions; a source missing from Danielsson is Eco (2005), whose research on myth and the series form highlights the ways in which the structure of a murder investigation has an impact on the construction of the protagonist.

In the following sections, I analyse the detective figure in contemporary crime fiction series and I propose a new theory that supersedes the findings of earlier critics. This Element is intended as a reference and source of inspiration for students, teachers, researchers, creative writers, and readers of crime fiction. In defining the terms used throughout my study, series is a collection of related but independent stories, whereas a serial is a single story divided into increments. Serial is also the adjectival form of series, and to avoid ambiguity around which literary mode is being referenced, I adopt the position of Jones and Walton, using 'series' as both noun and adjective. My concepts are evidenced via exemplary series across a range of subgenres: thriller, police procedural, neo-hardboiled, noir, private eye, and cosy crime; by authors including Lee

Child, Tana French, Sue Grafton, P.D. James, Katherine Kovacic, Attica Locke, Liza Marklund, Sujata Massey, Denise Mina, Walter Mosley, Barbara Neely, Sara Paretsky, Ian Rankin, and Ruth Rendell. These series are a representative selection but they also reflect the dual foundations of the current era, namely Golden Age and Hardboiled. As Danielsson points out, 'classic and hardboiled detective fiction have for a long time constituted the two main subgenres and the bases for many later sub-subgenres' (2002: 29).

My sample series are distinct in tone, style, setting, and themes, but they all adhere to the format of an investigative figure that solves a new crime in each successive novel. The contemporary approach is typified by Ian Rankin's police procedural set in Scotland, and I use his Inspector Rebus series as a benchmark, comparing it to other series chosen to highlight the arguments. My ideas are supported by author interviews, along with studies on crime fiction and other genres, and incorporating research on different media such as film and TV. I aim to decolonise, to question the binaries around gender, in order to rethink the crime series in ways that capture our modern world. By treating each series as a meganarrative and choosing authors that typify different facets of the form, I arrive at a set of propositions.

This Element reveals the character-shaping tendencies in the contemporary crime fiction series, and I demonstrate that the form produces a protagonist that is mythorealist. The concept is introduced in Section 2, where I scrutinise 'character' and show that the detective figure's realism is tempered by mythic structures, with the murder quest generating an on-duty/off-duty protagonist. Section 3 examines character consistency versus development, and mythorealism is presented in detail, unifying the ideas of Eco and Danielsson. Section 4 investigates the inevitable masculinity of the mythorealist detective figure, and I indicate how the performance of femininity can subvert this. In Section 5, I discuss the feminised protagonist and propose that mythorealism is a spectrum, ranging from mythic/masculinised figures to more feminised/realist figures. Section 6 looks at future trends, and the overall study concludes in Section 7 with my guide to writing a crime fiction series. This Element defines how the detective figure is made and maintained in the contemporary crime fiction series, and I also evaluate how these conventions can be adapted to innovate the genre and offer fresh insights on today's world and who we are.

2 Creating and Curating Character

The crime genre is associated with peril, pace, plot, intrigue, action, social commentary, vivid settings, the seduction of vicarious transgression, and the comfort of resolution. But when considering series, what first comes to mind is the lead character. We talk of the Perveen Mistry series, the Inspector Rebus series, the Easy Rawlins series, and the V.I. Warshawski series. This act of naming is significant: it identifies the character as the driving force in each crime series. To establish the ways in which mythorealism shapes these figures, I look at how their realism is expressed, and the initial indicators that this is influenced by mythic archetypes. Like a detective myself, in the following pages I investigate the eponymous protagonist, beginning with the fundamentals. What is meant by character? Who or what is being described?

The study of fictional character has its origins in the fourth century BCE, with Aristotle's *Poetics*, and many different interpretations have emerged since, evident in Heidbrink's detailed survey (2010). In the past sixty years the term 'character' has been a topic of entrenched debate: the formalist or structuralist approach treats literary character as an abstract concept or set of signs, whereas the humanist approach treats it as a real or human-like being. Pervading these definitions is how 'character' is understood in everyday terms. Taking as an example Ian Rankin's series, his protagonist Inspector Rebus is 'a character' in that he is a (fictional/invented) person in a novel. First published in 1987, there are twenty-five novels to date and the Rebus series belongs to the realist tradition in literature, in that it contains people and events one could encounter in the real world (as opposed to genres such as fantasy or science fiction, which may diverge from the known).

The character created by Rankin is given a particular name, John Rebus (usually referred to as Rebus), along with a set of attributes that define his outward presentation: male, Scottish, Police Detective, lives in Edinburgh, middle-aged, single or in a short-term relationship, dishevelled appearance, smoker, whisky drinker, and music lover. Turning to a few extracts that illustrate these attributes, in #2 *Hide and Seek* Rebus reflects on his recent break-up, 'Another notch in his bow of failed relationships' (2011b: 16); his routine at home is described, 'He would pour himself a drink, put some tenor sax music on' (59); in #13 *Resurrection Men* Rebus's smoking habit is referenced, 'He lit himself a cigarette, ignoring the No Smoking signs' (2001: 45). Some of these aspects change in later novels (from #18 onward Rebus is ostensibly a private investigator, after retiring from the police), but for most of the meganarrative the same outer attributes are encountered, albeit the descriptions will vary.

Rebus is the lead character in the series, but he is also depicted as possessing character; here the word is used in its other sense, signifying personality and the moral qualities distinctive to a (living) individual. A reader treats Rebus (a fictional figure) as if he has a rich mental landscape that could reflect their own. The novels relay Rebus's actions, his dialogue with different characters, and his inner monologue where he is shown thinking about himself or others and the world he inhabits. All these passages have a cumulative effect and the reader construes Rebus's inner character by piecing together all the references in the narrative. Rebus's attributes include loner, contrarian, brooding, volatile, pessimist, grim/ironic sense of humour, rule-breaker, avenger, and moralising/judgemental but aware of his own flaws: for instance the extract above where Rebus is shown as rule-breaker, 'ignoring the No Smoking signs'; or later in *Resurrection Men* when Rebus acknowledges his moral failings, '*This* was how the jobs got done: with a tainted conscience, guilty deals, and complicity' (Rankin, 2001: 427).

Throughout the series, the reader becomes acquainted and reacquainted with the main aspects of Rebus's inner character and Rankin is, whether consciously or not, adhering to an 'essentialist' metaphysics of human character, associated with the Western tradition. This concept can be traced to Plato and his theory that each object has an essence, a set of core qualities. When applied to human existence, this philosophy suggests that a (living) person has an inner essence, which dictates their actions and beliefs. In writing Rebus, Rankin creates a realist fictional figure that taps into ideas about what defines us as individuals. The outer attributes previously described (Scottish, Police Detective) are combined with the inner attributes conferred on Rebus (loner, contrarian), and together they become embedded, novel after novel, as characteristics, as the composite traits that identify Rebus.

There are similar processes evident in Katherine Kovacic's cosy crime series set in Australia, which generate the recognisable characteristics of protagonist Alex Clayton, who works as an art dealer. This leads to her involvement in a number of murder investigations, where Clayton's role becomes that of amateur detective. First published in 2018 there are currently three novels, making it shorter than the Rebus series, but the same principles apply. Present in the descriptions and dialogue, in the action scenes and moments of contemplation, are the qualities that identify Clayton. The protagonist's outer attributes include female, Australian, art dealer/expert, lives in Melbourne, long 'unruly' hair, owns an Irish wolfhound; for example, in #2 *Painting in the Shadows* Clayton refers to her appearance, 'I run a tired hand through my already mussed hair' (2019: loc. 1318). Turning to the protagonist's inner attributes, these include forthright, methodical, insightful, optimist, fearless, empathetic but with a teasing sense of humour; for example, in #3 *The Shifting Landscape* Clayton's methodical nature is apparent in her survey of the art collection in a wealthy homestead, 'The next couple of hours pass quickly as I work my way from room to room' (2020: 61).

Rankin and Kovacic have each created a memorable fictional character with certain traits. Returning to Danielsson's ideas, discussed in Section 1, these days a typical series protagonist will be equipped with 'a private life and personal problems' that unfold novel by novel in a format similar to a *roman fleuve* (2003: 1). Indeed, Rankin cites Anthony Powell's *A Dance to the Music of Time* as a crucial influence (Plain, 2002: 14). Rankin's Rebus and Kovacic's Clayton appear to reflect Danielsson's position that 'most contemporary detective series … resemble traditional, realistic novels in that psychological processes are part of the plot and developing characters are the sources of action' (2003: 2). While realism, and its associated focus on life story, is significant to interpreting the detective figure, it only offers a partial understanding.

Alongside a seeming realism, I argue that these characters are mythic, and there is evidence for this throughout their construction. One area where it emerges is in the repetition and recurrence that are intrinsic to the series form. Across a meganarrative such as Rankin's, the reader expects to recognise the same Rebus in each instalment. Naming the protagonist 'Rebus' is not enough, his identifying traits are required as confirmation, and in every novel Rebus comes equipped with his familiar physical and metaphysical 'baggage'. That the protagonist of a crime series will have certain habitual traits has always been a facet of the genre, and in Golden Age series they often took the form of stock phrases, such as 'little grey cells', the expression used by Agatha Christie's Hercule Poirot to describe his brain. The shift, in recent decades, toward greater realism has meant that these identifying traits have become more nuanced and yet they are still present. Danielsson proposes that 'most contemporary detective series … resemble traditional, realistic novels' but I argue that when these series are scrutinised with respect to the repeat performance, in each instalment, of the protagonist's identifying traits, then the resemblance to 'traditional, realistic novels' cannot be sustained.

It was Eco who recognised the significance of myth as well as structuring devices in the series form, and he was 'one of the first critics to take popular seriality seriously by emphasising the effectiveness of its oscillation between repetition and variation (or innovation) as a narrative forcefield' (Mayer, 2020: 32). Eco suggests that in crime series the reader 'continuously recovers, point by point, what he already knows, what he wants to know again' (2005: 159): in other words, the reader seeks repetition without much variation. Eco also proposes that 'Vices, gestures, nervous tics permit us to find an old friend in the character portrayed' (158). His observations were made in 1962 with respect to Rex Stout's Nero Wolfe series, which predates the drive toward a more realist detective figure with an ongoing biography. However, as argued by Vanacker, iteration remains crucial even in later series with a life-story structure, such as Sara Paretsky's series featuring private investigator V.I. Warshawski, which repeatedly offers the 'affirmation that the reader is encountering the same, unaltered, beloved character ... As a result each Warshawski novel iteratively performs Warshawski's personality' (2015: 101).

The repeat performance of 'the same, unaltered, beloved character' could turn Warshawski into the type of emblematic figure found in mythology, where iteration and multiple 'tellings' reinforce the protagonist's allegorical function as well as their durability. This tendency toward petrification is, to an extent, avoided by Paretsky through the portrayal of her protagonist as a realist figure, with a complex life that changes across the meganarrative. Similarly, in the series by Rankin and Kovacic, the petrification of the protagonist is offset by their 'realistic' lives: Rebus is shown negotiating the ongoing challenges of modern-day policing, alongside the ups and downs of personal relationships; Clayton encounters different facets of criminality in the art world, and the novels describe the dynamics of her relationship with her art conservator friend and would-be lover. As will become apparent, in these and other series examined in this Element, the detective figure is a negotiation between the retelling in each instalment of fixed traits, a mode associated with mythic archetypes, and the more variable biographic impulses associated with realism.

The Jack Reacher series offers a counterexample, with less evidence of realist variation, and instead mythic iteration comes to the fore. First published in 1997, there are twenty-four volumes authored by Lee Child, mostly set in the decades after Reacher leaves the army, becoming a 'drop-out' who roams the United States of America, delivering his version of justice. Each novel describes the protagonist's height (6'5"), weight (220–250lbs), eye colour (blue), and each novel demonstrates that he is exceptionally strong, a loner, rootless, fearless, and invincible. Time and again Reacher is shown single-handedly vanquishing a large group of assailants, such as in #16 *The Affair* (2012: 249–52). Child's novels are classed as thrillers, fast-paced and action-packed, but they often entail an investigation, and Reacher is a former military policeman. As noted by Sutton, 'The two branches of "crime" fiction – the thriller (basically, where action moves forward from one menacing, threatening, or murderous situation to the next) and the detective novel (where the investigation moves backward to uncover the crime and who did it) have variously merged and morphed' (2023: 64–5). This merging is apparent in Child's series, and Reacher is a combination of amateur/professional detective in a thriller format, where each investigation is pursued for personal reasons, using the character's military-police expertise, and culminating in Reacher killing his adversaries.

Unlike Rankin or Kovacic or other contemporary authors, Child avoids creating a chronological arc for his detective figure. The repeat performance of Reacher's identifying traits (height, strength, and invincibility), along with his apparent lack of a joined-up life story, show that Child's series is closer to the pre-biography mode examined by Eco (2005). In the Rebus and Clayton series, their inner and outer attributes are incorporated in ways that suffuse the narrative, and both characters seem real. In the Reacher series his attributes are emphasised and he presents as a mythic hero. Later in this study, I look in more detail at how the conventions can accommodate such a range. For now the key point is that in all three series, indeed in every contemporary crime fiction series, the repetition of identifying traits allows the author to convey the detective figure across each instalment of the meganarrative while maintaining their 'recognisability'. But as a consequence of these retellings, the realism of the detective figure inevitably adheres to mythic archetypes.

2.1 Reiterative Framing

So far I have examined how the iteration of traits is one of the techniques that generates the mythorealism of the protagonist. But repetition, as seen earlier, is partly about transporting a character across the duration of a meganarrative. This process is 'enabled' by the curation of consistent attributes, but there is a further strategy by which an author can sustain their lead character, through brief evocative scenes or vignettes that recur within each novel and throughout the series. There are repeating vignettes in Rankin's series, which include: Rebus's regular visits to the Oxford Bar; the moment when he inspects the lack of food in his kitchen; and his propensity to sleep in his living room. Such scenes relate to customary things a protagonist does, hence are likely to repeat. An author, I suggest, is not 'deliberately' framing their detective figure in a particular setting, instead the technique emerges as a byproduct of creating a character with certain habits.

To show the ways in which reiterative framing supports character creation and maintenance, I turn to the vignette of Rebus spending the night in his living room, for example, in #2 *Hide and Seek*: 'Sleep did not come easy, but eventually, slumped in his favourite chair, a book propped open on his lap, he must have dozed off' (Rankin, 2011b: 35). Later in the same novel there is another instance: 'Rebus opened his eyes. The sun was streaming into his living room, a record's run-out crackling. Another night spent in the chair, fully clothed' (177). In #13 *Resurrection Men* the motif appears again: 'Rebus sat down in his chair, prepared to let the night-time take its toll' (2001: 211).

Numerous examples could be cited from the Rebus meganarrative showing the protagonist asleep in his living room. Eco refers to the presence in crime series of a 'repertoire of *topoi*, of recurrent stock situations which animate these stories' (2005: 159), and I contend that the dual definition of topos is significant. A topos is a traditional theme or formula in literature but has its origins in the

Greek word for place. The vignette of Rebus sleeping in his chair does more than 'animate these stories'. The depiction of a series character in a particular locus or place is a way of relaying additional meanings. An insight on this process can be found in Jameson's study on Raymond Chandler, where he considers Barthes's theories about the reality effect or *effet de réel*, and the role of description in a text:

> If in Balzac the object-world was meant to give a metonymic signal, like a wild animal's den or an exoskeleton, in the Barthesian view of Flaubert's descriptions, these last were simply meant to emit the signal "we are the real, we are reality" – by virtue of their very contingency (their absence of necessity?). It was because such details (the ornate clock, the barometer) played no part in the action, and unlike their Balzacian equivalent did not mean or express anything, that they were able to stand in for the sheer massive contingency of reality itself (2016: 66).

I argue that in contemporary crime series the physical details that reiteratively frame the detective figure are transmitting a metonymic signal (Balzac's approach), but they also furnish the fictional world with the contingent 'stuff' (Flaubert's approach) that declares 'this is real'. Rebus's chair allows a reader to 'picture' his home, but the chair also emits a metonymic signal, communicating how alone the protagonist is, sleeping in his living room, rarely making it to bed, no family or spouse/partner influencing his habits. The chair also implies his nights are restless: Rebus is upright, devoid of comfort, 'Sleep did not come easy'. This vignette tells the reader, via a process of iteration, that not only is Rebus a loner, but he is also a troubled loner.

A connection can be made, I suggest, between this technique and how figures from myth are portrayed in visual representations: for example, in early Greek ceramics a wounded male figure shackled to a stake or a cliff face would be recognised as Prometheus, one of the Titans from Greek mythology, because of how he is reiteratively framed in a particular setting. These methods, associated with the communication of mythic archetypes in the visual arts, have affinities with the textual techniques evident in crime series. The detective figure is depicted in a situation/setting that becomes emblematic, and this is apparent in Kovacic's series, which contains a recurring motif of the protagonist standing before a painting and letting it 'speak' to her. The vignette conveys Clayton's expertise within the art world, the character's ability to analyse and interpret:

> I pause in front of John Brack's *The Block*. There is something deeply disturbing about that empty butcher's shop. It is totally devoid of life, except for the hulking presence of a dark chopping block standing in front of a closed coolroom door. The starkness of the scene is heightened by Brack's smooth

> application of paint, and there is a clinical quality to his sharp lines that contrive to turn an empty room into a visceral scream (2019: loc. 1332).

This passage of ekphrasis is in #2 *Painting in the Shadows*, but across the series there are many encounters with art. They present Clayton as able to find deeper meanings beneath the painted surface. The vignette reinforces why Clayton has the skills to catch a killer, as she can 'see' beneath someone's outward appearance and uncover their true intentions. And such validation is arguably necessary as Clayton is an amateur detective, whose credentials need proving.

These vignettes, in the Rebus and Clayton novels, contribute to the maintenance of series characters through the staging of their identifying traits in particular locations. The techniques examined so far are all associated with establishing, in each successive novel, that it is the 'same' detective figure. Across the multiple instalments of a meganarrative, character consistency becomes a central concern. The identifying traits typically operate within certain parameters, an aspect Rosen notes in relation to another genre:

> a character's field cannot be shifted to an unlimited degree. In fan fiction, a character like Captain Kirk might have a different sexual orientation or might be the manager of a Starbucks instead of a starship, but he would not resemble the Kirk we know at all if he were an uninsured part-time barista at that same Starbucks and talked like Spock (2016: 177–8).

These observations are applicable to a single-authored meganarrative such as a crime series. Based on the premise that 'a character's field cannot be shifted to an unlimited degree', a reader, after just one Rebus novel, will expect to meet a sufficiently similar Rebus in the next novel. If he were portrayed as a cheerful optimist, the reader might suspect a substitution. Iterative traits thereby become a way of announcing and curating the Rebusness of Rebus, his fictional quiddity. Similarly, in Kovacic's series, if Clayton stopped being devoted to her wolfhound Hogarth, then the reader would think 'this is not the Clayton I know'.

The reiteration of identifying traits, alongside repeating vignettes, are two of the principal ways in which an author can transport their protagonist from novel to novel, while maintaining the consistency and recognisability desired by the reader. Such aspects promote a durable mythic archetype, but this tendency to remain static is then effectively offset by the realism of the protagonist's ongoing life story. These initial conclusions support my theory that the series form generates a detective figure that is part mythic, part realist. Turning now to the ways in which murder shapes the protagonist, I will establish what else mythorealism brings to the series form.

2.2 On-Duty/Off-Duty

In crime series featuring a detective figure, the investigation of crime is the main thrust of the plot in each novel. The crime is typically a violent death. The stakes are high and the protagonist is put under extreme duress: can they catch the killer, will the killer strike again, how dangerous is the investigation, will the protagonist become the next victim? Across all genres, including literary fiction, the pressures directed at the lead character, and the need for them to react to events or dictate what happens, are arguably what motivate the unfolding narrative. Causal impulses and propulsive effects are nearly always present in literature. But crime fiction is where the influence of duress is most clearly discernible and generically encoded. These are brutal narratives where the consequences are death, not hurt feelings.

It is this extreme duress that gives rise to what is, I contend, one of the truly distinctive features of crime series character: the protagonist only appears on the page when there is an instigating crime, typically murder, which triggers the next novel in the sequence. In my interview with Rankin, I asked, 'Is Rebus's light switched off when there's no crime, is his voice silenced?' He responded:

> the murder rate in Edinburgh isn't huge, and so, when I was writing the books, I kind of thought, well, this is the one exciting thing that happens to him the whole year. So each book is basically a year of his life. Although the events of the book might only take place over eight, ten days ... And the rest of the year's been a bit more banal. It's been bland, banal, boring, nothing much happening ... they're just being cops going about their normal business, and investigating easily solved, domestic-style cases, that aren't very interesting to read about (Rankin, 2016).

Rebus is brought to life when there is a violent and 'exciting' crime to solve, but deprived of agency during the 'bland, banal, boring' rest of the year. The text falls silent between novels when there is 'nothing much happening', but this pattern is also apparent within the novels, where Rebus's weekends (his time off) are also depicted as 'bland, banal, boring', for example, in #13 *Resurrection Men*:

> He'd spent most of Saturday in the Oxford Bar, passing time first with one set of drinkers, then with another. Finally, he'd headed back to his flat and fallen asleep in the chair, waking at midnight with a raging thirst and a thumping head. He'd not been able to get back to sleep until dawn, meaning he didn't wake until midday on Sunday. A visit to the launderette had filled in the afternoon, and he'd gone back to the Ox in the evening (Rankin, 2001: 75).

Once again Rebus is shown sleeping in a chair, but the aspect I wish to stress is how two (fictional) days have been reduced to one paragraph, in stark contrast to Rebus's crime-centred working week, where a single day may fill several chapters. In *Resurrection Men* Rebus is investigating a group of corrupt police officers, the cold-case murder of a Glasgow gangster, and the recent murder of an Edinburgh art dealer. These topics dominate the novel and the narrative directs the reader to privilege the on-duty presentation of the protagonist, disregarding his off-duty hours.

The text also pays little attention to the undramatised lacunae between the Rebus novels, the eleven and a half months that comprise the rest of the fictional year. Those gaps are unwritten, but the implication is that Rebus continues working ('investigating easily solved, domestic-style cases') and continues going to the Oxford Bar, but that there is nothing worth 'sharing' with the reader until the advent of another complex murder enquiry, instigating the next novel. There are occasional references to these 'between' times, such as the following from #2 *Hide and Seek* where Rebus alludes to his wife and daughter: 'They had grown so far apart, ever since Rhona had taken Samantha to live in London' (Rankin, 2011b: 15). This describes events that happen 'unseen' between #1 and #2. The demise of Rebus's marriage could provide content for a whole novel, but instead, the topic is consigned to the interstices as there is no murder to elicit its inclusion. A further instance of between time can be found in #13 *Resurrection Men*, when Rebus recalls a period back before the series started: 'Memories of his marriage and the day he had moved into the Arden Street flat with his young wife ... newly married and with a first-time mortgage, Rhona talking about kids' (Rankin, 2001: 75).

These extracts show Rebus contemplating events that are situated outside the immediate concerns of the novel. Fictionalised self-reflection is not, however, a strong component of Rankin's series. Section 5 considers a number of counterexamples, but on the whole detective figures such as Rankin's Inspector Rebus or Kovacic's Alex Clayton or Child's Jack Reacher rarely have time to ponder their existence because they are too busy catching killers. Their attention is focused on the 'quest' to solve the murder or major crime(s), this teleologically oriented arc being a defining feature of the genre. As Malmgren states, 'Crime fictions are quest narratives' in which 'someone is looking for someone or something' (2010: 152). Quest narratives are present in different mythologies from across the globe, a topic I return to, but the key point here is how murder shapes the protagonist: it 'awakens' the detective figure, and the subsequent narrative is then focused on their efforts to solve that murder.

2.3 Action versus Introspection

In contemporary crime series the quest is typically to right a perceived wrong, either through legal/professional means (Rankin's Rebus series), through amateur detection (Kovacic's Clayton series), or through illegal/vigilante methods (Child's Reacher series). With a quest as the driving force in each novel, when 'thinking' is depicted it is usually associated with unravelling the murder. The protagonist's inner monologue will be directed at deciphering clues, evaluating leads, and assessing potential culprits via techniques such as psychological profiling. Thinking is rarely idle musing: finding the killer requires focused analysis and action. Rankin's series portrays Rebus as needing to be active rather than introspective, for example, in #13 *Resurrection Men* where he rejects the idea of living in the countryside: 'he feared the silence would get to him eventually, drawing him deeper into himself – not a place he really wanted to be' (2001: 307). Rebus is shown to prefer the bustle of city life and his restlessness mirrors the narrative structure, which promotes an active protagonist whose energies are directed at apprehending criminals. Murder is the catalyst that turns 'bland, banal, boring' Rebus into the obsessive, tormented figure that will pursue a killer until they are caught, regardless of personal consequences:

> It was two in the morning when the phone woke him. He was lying on the living room floor, next to the hi-fi, CD cases and album sleeves spread around him. He crawled on hands and knees to his chair and picked up the receiver ... 'How soon can you get down here?' Hogan was asking.
> 'Depends where "here" is.' Rebus was doing a stock-check: head cloudy but bearable; stomach queasy (Rankin, 2001: 330).

This extract is three-quarters of the way into *Resurrection Men*. Rebus is not accorded the (relative) comfort of falling asleep in his favourite chair, instead he is lying on the floor, his 'head cloudy but bearable; stomach queasy'. From the start of the novel onward, Rebus is shown to suffer increasing levels of mental anguish, and in the finale he is physically assaulted, requiring 'a blood transfusion and seven stitches' (436). At the end of each Rebus novel, once the investigation concludes, this heightened, transfigured, and tormented version of the character subsides and leaves. In #2 *Hide and Seek* Rebus's withdrawal is staged across two pages, which culminate with the protagonist holding a lit match (2011b: 261): will Rebus burn the incriminating photographs? The question remains open, and there is none of the knot-tying closure of Golden Age detective fiction. On departing the text Rebus is delivered into an unnarrated limbo where doubts and recriminations linger. And from this same limbo the character is summoned once more, at the start of the next novel in the series.

A similar structure is apparent in Kovacic's series. The novels only 'happen' when Clayton's work as an art dealer brings her into proximity with violent death, for example, in #3 *The Shifting Landscape* when she is employed to value the art collection of a wealthy farming family and the patriarch is murdered the day of her arrival. Only when compelled by circumstance does Clayton emerge from limbo and adopt the (part-time) role of amateur detective. The series is not concerned with the run-of-the-mill rest of her existence as there is no crime demanding an account. Critics such as Danielsson suggest that contemporary crime fiction series are extended biographies, but I argue that the evidence says otherwise.

When I examine the material included in contemporary crime series, it leads me to one conclusion: these are records of the protagonist's involvement in murder quests, and huge portions of their lives are omitted. Such omissions are very apparent in the Reacher series, which Child acknowledges as a deliberate ploy: 'I want, in the reader's head, Reacher's voice to be silenced between adventures in order to emphasise that, sure, for three hundred and sixty-four days of the year, nothing happens to him, he does not stumble into trouble' (Child, 2018). Reacher is a drifter and 'when he had to he worked whatever job he could get. He had worked the doors in night clubs, and he had dug swimming pools, and stacked lumber, and demolished buildings, and picked apples' (2013: 151). However, these activities never feature in the novels.

Reacher does not become the character associated with Reacher until he 'stumble[s] into trouble', for example, in #14 *61 Hours*. The protagonist is travelling by coach through South Dakota, not engaging with other passengers: 'his responses . . . courteous but brief' (2010b: 22). When the coach crashes they are all taken to a police station, where Reacher glimpses crime-scene photographs of a 'sprawled black-clad body, large, probably male, probably dead' (50). Reacher becomes much more engaged, telling the Police Chief, 'I like to know things. I'm hungry for knowledge' (57). The protagonist is once again on-duty, the super-charged 'twin' who surfaces once or twice a year for an action-packed 500 pages. In *61 Hours* the police ask Reacher to protect an elderly librarian who is witness to a drug deal. After a corrupt officer arranges her assassination, Reacher embarks on a mission to exterminate the gang, who have been selling World-War-Two methamphetamines, stored in a nuclear bunker. This is the Reacher familiar to readers, and yet for most of his supposed 'life' he is the other Reacher we never see. Once each quest is completed, Reacher withdraws from the text and from society, as exemplified by the ending to #1 *Killing Floor*: 'I didn't want property taxes and maintenance and chambers of commerce . . . I wanted the open road and a new place every day' (2010a: 523).

In the Rebus and Clayton and Reacher meganarratives there is a repeating pattern, whereby a dormant character is activated at the start of each novel. As previously discussed, patterning is one of the ways in which mythic archetypes enter the crime series form. Before proceeding to my definition of mythorealism in Section 3, I consider the wider inferences that can be drawn from the findings amassed so far. The crime series is a literary form that engages with ideas about what constitutes 'existence'. I argue that the modulation of the series protagonist, through dormancy and activation, reflects a conception of human character relating to 'hypokeimenon', and I turn to Gadamer for a definition: 'This word means "that which underlies." One finds the word in Aristotelian physics and metaphysics, and in such contexts it has a long history in Latin, as *substantia* or as *subiectum*. Both of these are Latin translations of *hypokeimenon*, which is, and means, that which remains unchanged as it underlies the process of all change' (2000: 276).

This theory does not originate in literary criticism but relates to philosophical enquiries, during Greco-Roman antiquity, on the nature of existence, where everything was recognised as possessing a set of core qualities. Keane and Lawn suggest that hypokeimenon 'articulates the unchanging substratum that underlies every change or alteration' (2011: 138). In its Latin translation as subiectum and the variation subjectum, we see the origins of the term 'subject', which among its current definitions can mean a person or topic being discussed, as well as a thinking, feeling entity. I contend that the metaphysical model of character present in crime series is that of a latent subjectum, intermittently catalysed by violence into becoming the active subject on the pages of the novel. A murder summons the protagonist from dormancy, the quest commits them to take action, and the narrative is a record of those actions.

I have already established that the creation and maintenance of a series protagonist (via the iteration of identifying traits) draws upon an essentialist understanding of human character, dating back to Plato. My discussion of hypokeimenon, along with subjectum/subject, indicates how the underlying/identifying traits then relate to the protagonist being catalysed into performing them. In crime series, these ideas inherited from Western antiquity are brought into counterpoint (via the imperative to 'take action') with a diametrically opposed concept, namely the existential model of human character. Associated with European philosophers of the nineteenth- and twentieth-centuries, it is based on the belief that who we are is determined by what actions we choose to take in this world, with our identity then being shaped by the cumulative accretion of such acts of free will.

If I take these different ways of interpreting a person's being, and apply them to the crime series studied here, the protagonist can be viewed as a carefully curated character with a set of traits that keep repeating (reflecting essentialist ideas), but at the same time the activated protagonist is defined by the sum total of what they do in each novel (reflecting existentialist ideas). Does the interplay of ancient and modern metaphysics offer guidance on what makes a detective figure? I argue that the elusiveness of such a figure, its situatedness in the tension in-between, is an intrinsic quality, and the concept of 'character' created by these fictions will always defy any rigid taxonomy. Nevertheless, the relationship between subjectum/subject and essentialist/existentialist models does narrow down the territory where, within an ontology of fictional being, one can locate the crime series protagonist. Philosophy and metaphysics have shed light on this territory, but to further my understanding, I once again turn to myth, another mode of enquiry that has sought to interpret who we are. The pattern created in crime series, of a character who springs into action to pursue a quest, is threaded through with ancient storytelling traditions. Coupe describes myth as 'an elemental expression of the narrative imagination' (2010: xi), and in the following section I establish the key features associated with the merging of realism and myth that have generated the contemporary detective figure.

3 Mythorealism

Mythorealism is the term I have coined for my theory about the contemporary crime fiction series. It is fundamental to an understanding of the detective figure: a character who obeys certain predetermined patterns and yet whose destiny is also unforeseeable. Mythorealism constructs an immortal and heroic protagonist who rises from the ashes when required to solve a crime, who is pushed to the limit in each novel, often risking life and limb, and who is seemingly undaunted by a long history of violent events, with little or no memory of past trauma. This same protagonist also appears to be mortal and equipped with an ongoing biography and a realist existence, comprising events in their (minimal) personal life together with (suppressed) events connected to each previous murder investigation.

Throughout Section 3, I present evidence to support my definition of mythorealism, beginning with how 'change' is modelled in the protagonist. As noted by Danielsson, the biographic structure in crime series means that current authors tend to place more emphasis on the detective figure developing in ways that reflect real life, through the ageing process and psychological maturing. Such changes may seem at odds with the fixity of myth, but even here there is evidence of how the two modes combine. I established in Section 2 that murder (or a major crime) is the catalyst that brings the protagonist out of limbo. These rebirths have the predestiny of myth, but they also allow the detective figure to alter with each new iteration. In discussing his Inspector Rebus series, author Ian Rankin states: 'I've never felt, as I start to write a novel, oh here we are going through the motions again, because between books

[Rebus] has changed, so I'm not writing about the same guy twice' (Rankin, 2016). In an early novel, *Hide and Seek*, the protagonist is introduced via a dinner party scene in Chapter One: 'John Rebus stared hard at the dish in front of him, oblivious to the conversation around the table ... an unfocussed despair grew within him' (Rankin, 2011b: 2). This passage can be juxtaposed with the opening sentences of later novel *Resurrection Men*:

> 'Then why are you here?'
> 'Depends what you mean,' Rebus said.
> 'Mean?' The woman frowned behind her glasses.
> 'Mean by "here",' he explained. 'Here in this
>   room? Here in this career? Here on the planet?'
> (Rankin, 2001: 1).

Over a decade of (fictional) time has passed between #2 and #13, and my comparison shows how Rebus has seemingly changed and matured, from mute, despairing Rebus in *Hide and Seek* to confident, dry-witted Rebus in *Resurrection Men*. The physical ageing of Rebus is also depicted in the novels. The character is forty-one years old in #1 *Knots and Crosses* (Rankin, 2011a: 31), and across the series he goes from being a middle-aged but relatively youthful figure, able to knock an opponent unconscious (2011b: 248), to a man in his late sixties with a chronic health condition, who struggles to climb a stair (2019: 13).

There are other strategies by which a detective figure can be developed. The length of a series creates opportunities for further insights on the character's 'psyche', for example, when Rebus has a moment of self-awareness in #5 *The Black Book*: 'He thought about the job too much as it was, gave himself to it the way he had never given himself to any *person* in his life' (Rankin, 2011c: 93). Another technique for disclosing more about a series character is through the inclusion, in selected novels, of elements from a protagonist's backstory, such as the passage quoted in Section 2, where Rebus recalls the early days of his marriage (2001: 75). These methods effectively signal within the text the mortal part of the mythorealist detective figure.

Change means that new aspects are added to the protagonist as the meganarrative progresses, with some of this material being deferred to later instalments. The concept of narrative deferral has, to date, provided a tool for analysing how the content of these crime novels is structured to produce mystery and intrigue, Levay noting 'the pleasures of detective fiction ... arise from a process of narrative deferral, a continued suspense that comes when one resists the urge to predict a plot's outcome and instead follows the twists of a complex, unfolding narrative' (2019: 147). I suggest this process also applies to the protagonist. The possibility of fully knowing the detective figure is always postponed to the next novel in the sequence. This entices the reader to continue their elusive quest to understand the main character, albeit that understanding remains out of reach, in the unwritten future. Situating this within literary theory, I argue that the narrative deferral in contemporary crime series generates the concept of fictional character as an entity that is yet to be fully known. The staged revelation of understanding, of answers and resolutions, can be seen to operate at two different scales within contemporary crime series. The reader wants to know how the murder in each novel will be solved, but they also want to know how the protagonist's personal life will develop across the meganarrative.

However, not all contemporary series feature protagonists that develop and mature. Some put less emphasis on the realism of a biographic arc, as evident in Lee Child's series with ex-military policeman/drifter Jack Reacher. Time does not seem to age Reacher, nor does lived experience affect his psyche. Child's protagonist displays character density as opposed to character development. Repurposing a phrase coined by Creeber (2004: 5), I argue that 'character density' is the property that defines detective figures prior to the 1970s, where narrative material accrues around a series protagonist but the words gravitate toward the same repeating behaviours. Reacher is modelled using this earlier technique, reflecting Child's belief that 'the reader wants the same guy to show up each time' (2018). Nowadays however, the majority of contemporary protagonists, such as Ian Rankin's Inspector Rebus, Sara Paretsky's V.I. Warshawski, and Katherine Kovacic's Alex Clayton, are more dynamic in their characterisation, with the incorporation of ageing and psychological maturing across the series arc.

Contemporary detective figures are shown to develop but, as discussed in Section 2, the techniques associated with curating a series protagonist, such as consistent traits and reiterative framing, will always entail an element of density. This density supports the mythic aspect of the detective figure, through the multiple retellings of a core set of traits and behaviours. As will become apparent, there is an inevitable tension between this seeming requirement for consistency and the trend toward character development.

3.1 Character Development

In contemporary crime fiction series, authors use two main methods to develop their detective figure, as evident in the examples discussed so far. The first technique is to include indicators, spread through the meganarrative, of physical and psychological maturing. This I term 'chronological development'. The second technique is to insert, at intervals in the novels, moments of self-awareness, and flashbacks to formative events in the past. This I term 'development by disclosure'. Rankin uses both approaches in his Rebus series, a meganarrative that spans three decades of the protagonist's existence, and nearly four decades of the author's life.

The same strategies are also present in series with fewer instalments, such as Sujata Massey's cosy crime series, first published in 2018. There are four novels featuring Perveen Mistry, an Indian lawyer during the era of British colonial rule in India, and she fits my category of semi-professional detective. In #1 *The Widows of Malabar Hill* much of the narrative takes place in 1921 when Mistry investigates a murder related to a contentious will. However, there are chapters set in 1916 which show a younger Mistry who, raised in a progressive Parsi family, is unprepared for the loss of autonomy following her orthodox marriage (146–163). The flashback chapters depict a nineteen-year-old woman 'with more passion than sense' (147), in love with her betrothed. The novel also presents how the protagonist has changed: having separated from her abusive, unfaithful husband, Mistry declares, 'I know the pain of betrayal' (357), and she appears 'a touch older than twenty-three', with eyes 'more tired than merry' (63).

It is now common for series authors to apply both methods, chronological as well as by disclosure, to develop their detective figure. The amount of change is a matter of choice. For example in Sue Grafton's series, featuring private investigator Kinsey Millhone, there are twenty-five novels published between 1982 and 2017, but the author limits Millhone's chronological development: the protagonist only ages by ten years, even though thirty-five years have passed, such that later volumes become works of 'historical' fiction. There is enough flexibility in the series form to accommodate Grafton's approach, along with Child's denial of change, discussed earlier. However, the majority of contemporary authors calibrate their series on a chronology approximating to real time, with a new instalment published each year, and the detective figure slowly ageing/maturing.

The unfolding biography of the protagonist is one of the ways that the contemporary crime series appears to mimic human existence. The dynamics of personal relationships, along with the effects of ageing and psychological maturing, are consistent with writing a character that imitates real life. However, even under the scrutiny of editors, an author may create contradictions. Rankin acknowledges the inconsistency, between #5 and #10, to where Rebus attended school: 'In using my own life as a template for some of Rebus's background, errors sometimes do creep in' (2006: 6).

Along with unintended mistakes, there is another type of inconsistency that may reflect the author's deliberate or subconscious desire to evolve their protagonist. Vanacker observes that P.D. James's Inspector Adam Dalgliesh becomes less 'irritable' across the series arc (2011: 75). Dalgliesh also 'sheds the sexist comments of the earlier novels' (75), indicative of progress in societal attitudes during the publication timespan (1962–2008). These inconsistencies seem about altering rather than ageing the protagonist, but Vanacker contends: 'Dalgliesh's status as a character of long duration prevents us from seeing these minor changes as inconsistent. He resembles his readers, and his creator, in the sense that he appears to have slowly changed and aged over the decades' (75).

The length of these meganarratives is such that (deliberate) inconsistencies can be re-presented as compatible with character development. However, altering a character could cause the reader to question their authenticity. In series, the tendency is that any inconsistency will inflect but not transform the detective figure. It may be confined to one instalment, for example #11 of Child's series, *Bad Luck and Trouble,* when $1030 is deposited in Reacher's bank account, a curiously specific figure that prompts a bravura display of mental arithmetic: 'Square root? Clearly just a hair more than 32. Cube root? A hair less than 10.1'. This leads Reacher to the realisation, 'If a military policeman needs urgent assistance from a colleague he calls in a ten-thirty radio code' (2007: 13–14).

Maths-prodigy Reacher in #11 differs from other less gifted Reachers in the series, and Rabinowitz observes a similar issue in cartoon series: 'Are all the Bugs Bunnies, for instance, virtuoso pianists of the same caliber as the one in "Rhapsody Rabbit"?' (2002: 2). I argue that when enough identifying traits are maintained alongside these inconsistencies, such that the reader still 'recognises' Reacher, Rebus, Mistry, Dalgleish (or indeed Bugs Bunny), then the crime series form can accommodate inconsistencies: it allows unintended errors to be absorbed, and permits the trialling/testing of new attributes, that may or may not be retained in subsequent novels.

Now that character development has become a feature of most crime series, this creates a potential rupture. On one side are the stable traits associated with character density and the pre-determination of myth. On the other side are the variable aspects associated with character development and the unpredictability of real life. A character could change so radically across a meganarrative as to shed the stable traits of earlier novels, thereby becoming 'someone else'. However, apparent across the genre, these changes rarely take the protagonist on an extreme trajectory. Reader expectations are a factor. Once a series is underway, the familiar features of the detective figure tend to be maintained. Alter them too much, and it may alienate readers. However, do these protagonists change enough given the events they have seemingly lived through?

3.2 Amnesia

In contemporary series, I argue that crime and the novel are conjoined in a single system for the formation and re-formation of character. Here I rephrase Miller's analysis of Dickens's *Oliver Twist*: 'Police and offenders are conjoined in a single system for the formation and re-formation of delinquents' (1988: 5). Miller's study on nineteenth-century literature highlights 'the possibility of a radical *entanglement* between the nature of the novel and the practice of the police' (2). In contemporary crime series, I also observe an entanglement related to the subject matter of these narratives. Crime series contain the sorts of pressures that would tend to re-form character. The detective figure is at the centre of a murder investigation, exposed to death, depravity, and danger. The series form, as previously discussed, is equipped to model change and it could show the cumulative mental and physical toll on the protagonist, exerted by their proximity to violent crime. And yet in many contemporary series, the author curtails the trajectory of their detective figure and conserves their stable traits.

Certain methods are being used, within these fictions, to diffuse and disperse the potential 'harms' to the protagonist. The primary technique is amnesia. The deliberate forgetting or downplaying of past trauma allows the detective figure to carry on, unencumbered by grim remembrance. In Rankin's series, Rebus is rarely shown recalling the dire events of previous novels. In #1 *Knots and Crosses* his daughter is kidnapped and Rebus is shot and nearly strangled to death, and yet #2 *Hide and Seek* only mentions this briefly, and elliptically, when Rebus describes his promotion to Detective Inspector, following 'a long, hard case full of personal suffering' (2011b: 16). In Massey's series, the protagonist also elides previous incidents. In #4 *The Mistress of Bhatia House*, Mistry refers to #1 *The Widows of Malabar Hill* when she tells a client/friend: '"I've met DI Vaughan." It had been on a case where he'd bungled things so badly that women might have died if Perveen hadn't intervened' (Massey, 2023: 190). The word 'intervened' in #4 bypasses a fuller acknowledgement of the arduous investigation conducted by Mistry in #1. Nor is there any hint that Mistry also 'might have died' during the finale of #1. A reader of Massey's series would retain a memory of the challenges and dangers of previous instalments. Mistry, however, is presented as having a reductive recollection.

Series narratives are complex constructions and there are often multiple reasons why certain conventions have arisen. I suggest the lack of detail about past investigations allows the author to avoid 'spoilers' that reveal the finale of those earlier novels. Readers may not encounter a series in chronological order. Later instalments are usually circumspect about previous investigations, so that discoveries can be made even when the novels are read out of sequence. There are counterexamples, such as Bridget Walsh's Variety Palace Mysteries, where greater cohesion and continuity are created across the different volumes, and the reader is more likely to approach them in sequential order. This indicates that character amnesia is not a prerequisite of the form, but it is nevertheless a convention apparent in many contemporary crime series.

When considering other reasons why amnesia has emerged as a technique, I argue that it is allied with maintaining pace in the narrative. As a series grows in length, the constant recounting of a list of previous investigations, together with an extended summary of the character's personal life, would involve inserting a lot of backstory. With the shift toward a life-story structure, there is potential for a series to become burdened by its own past, apparent in Walter Mosley's series featuring private investigator Easy Rawlins. A crossover between the neo-hardboiled/noir subgenres, it was first published in 1990. The meganarrative spans a long retrospective and revisionist arc, with #1 set in 1948 and #15 set in the late 1960s. Mosley's series is highly innovative, a topic I return to in Section 5. However, the later Rawlins novels do exhibit certain narratological drawbacks. Each instalment presents a compelling plot but, as the series progresses, the protagonist acquires an increasingly complicated 'history' associated with past investigations as well as his ever-changing personal and family circumstances. Later novels contain passages summarising that backstory, the effect being to slow the pace and deplete the tension. One such example, in the first chapter of #13 *Rose Gold*, offers an abridged account of some of Rawlins's history:

> Five months or so earlier I had almost died. At that time I had been involved in a case that put my home in jeopardy, and so I had sent my daughter to stay with her brother at a friend's place, temporarily. I resolved the case but then drove my car off the side of a coastal mountain (Mosley, 2015: 1–2).

This terse summary of #11 is followed by a summary of #12, by which point the reader is up to date. The expositional tone of these paragraphs, full of information about past events, is inclined to distance the reader from the more immediate concerns of #13, an effect that is particularly noticeable because these are the opening pages and one is looking to be pulled into the narrative, rather than disengaged. Mosley's Easy Rawlins series is, however, atypical.

In the majority of contemporary series, the forward momentum of the prose is maintained by excluding any detailed accounts of incidents from earlier novels. This tendency is amplified in Child's Jack Reacher series where, as previously discussed, the past is effectively omitted. The issue of fictionalised forgetfulness is touched on by Richardson, who suggests that in genres with weaker mimetic pretensions, such as low-budget television series, 'there is no historical memory; detective Columbo doesn't remember getting knocked unconscious 50 times, or that the villain he faces has an identical modus operandi to a very similar villain he faced two years ago in viewing time' (2010: 535).

Reacher's 'mimetic pretensions' are not as weak as those of a character such as Columbo. There are small intimations that the protagonist does have a 'historical memory', but the experiences Reacher has seemingly lived through would test most mortal's endurance. The Reacher in #1 is a thirty-six-year-old, ex-army drifter. The Reacher in #24 is well into his fifties and still administering rough justice. The meganarrative portrays him as miraculously unaffected by a lifetime of hyper-violence. To treat Reacher as a real person presents a challenge. Child's protagonist is an outlying example, but this same imperviousness to the past is seen across the genre and it further dismantles Danielsson's notion that 'most contemporary detective series … resemble traditional, realistic novels' (2003: 2).

3.3 Mortal Meets Mythic

When reading an extended contemporary crime fiction series such as Rankin's Inspector Rebus, but also evident in shorter series such as Massey's Perveen Mistry novels, the protagonist changes and matures in ways that mimic real life. I have highlighted, in this section and those preceding, aspects of character construction which show the mortal and mythic being fused, but much of my discussion has centred on the 'human' part of the detective figure. These meganarratives put a lot of emphasis on the characters being believably real, but in Child's Jack Reacher the mythic underpinnings are exposed. Reacher's height, his muscled physique, and his capacity to win fights against multiple opponents, are the outward signs of mythic traits that determine his characterisation. Eco proposes:

> The hero equipped with powers superior to those of the common man has been a constant of the popular imagination … Often the hero's virtue is humanized, and his powers, rather than being supernatural, are the extreme realization of natural endowments, such as astuteness, swiftness, fighting ability, or even in the logical faculties and the pure spirit of observation found in Sherlock Holmes (2005: 146).

Throughout the series Reacher manifests the 'extreme realization of natural endowments', such as advanced analytical abilities and exceptional combat skills. His powers never diminish even as he notionally ages across the novels. An unchanging mythic hero is the inevitable outcome of a series where the protagonist's superior attributes are repeatedly performed in semi-identical circumstances. Reacher is figured as partly human, occasionally fallible, but mostly he is shown being invincible, the capacity to endure and vanquish thereby signalling his 'immortality'. I have already indicated that Child's series is an exception to recent trends, but even in more typical series the protagonist will summon superhuman abilities at key moments: for instance Alex Clayton, when she and her wolfhound are shot at (Kovacic, 2020: 185–7); or Perveen Mistry, who throws herself at the knife-wielding murderer in order to protect a young girl (Massey, 2018: 359–60).

That the detective figure has a mythic dimension has been noted by critics such as Munt (2004: 1), but to this I add my own findings, related to the amnesia discussed earlier. A crime series generates a protagonist who undergoes trauma in each successive novel, and yet they seem immune to harm. Amnesia removes the accumulated suffering that would, several decades into a series, make the reader question the believability of the protagonist. However, I contend that it creates a paradox unique to the detective figure in contemporary crime series: amnesia helps maintain the character's realism, and plausibility, by avoiding drawing the reader's attention to events they were subjected to in previous novels; but amnesia also serves to undermine the character's realism, by presenting them as impervious to their own past. Unlike most people in real life, these characters are rarely 'damaged' by the experiences they have seemingly undergone. I argue that the convention in contemporary crime series, whereby an author attributes a degree of amnesia to their protagonist, is part of what constructs the detective figure as mythic.

To determine what else myth brings to the series form, I turn to a number of definitions. As cited earlier, Coupe describes myth as 'an elemental expression of the narrative imagination' (2010: xi). Moyers, inspired by the ideas of Joseph Campbell (indebted to Vladimir Propp), sees myth as an expression of the 'need for life to signify, to touch the eternal, to understand the mysterious, to find out who we are' (Campbell & Moyers, 1991: 4). Numerous mythologies have emerged, across time, in cultures and regions all over the globe, including but not restricted to: Mesoamerican, Norse, Egyptian, Greek, West-African, Slavic, Japanese, and Māori. These predominantly oral traditions often contain mythic heroes that embody elemental yearnings to understand, through storytelling, who we are, our place on earth, and the nature of existence.

Inheritances from these mythic figures are, I contend, reflected in the crime series protagonist, and they account for my own life-long fascination with the detective: a figure that is more than human, but which reveals what it is to be human. There are instances of mythology and folklore having a direct influence on the genre, evident in Soitos's research on African American detective fiction. In his discussion of double-consciousness, he suggests this allows 'characters to assume identities and masks in the trickster tradition, hide their detective personas behind their blackness, and use hoo-doo powers in their detective work' (1996: 69); the trickster being a key figure in folklores which, through the appalling practices of the Atlantic slave trade, were brought to the United States in previous centuries by enslaved black people from Africa.

Along with how myth has, in various ways, shaped the protagonist in contemporary crime series, it is apparent too in the narrative form. Earlier, I referred to Malmgren's observation that 'Crime fictions are quest narratives' (2010: 152). Quests feature in many different mythologies, and it was Campbell (1973) who identified, through comparison of myths from a wide variety of cultures, the basic structure of 'the hero's journey' or monomyth, where the protagonist overcomes obstacles, leading to an ordeal in which the enemy is vanquished. As will be discussed in Section 5, this interpretation of quest as conquest is being reconceived by a number of innovative authors, but Campbell's theory still has relevance to my overall argument. In the traditional monomyth, found in these oral narratives, the hero is transformed by their journey. In the crime series, however, there is a crucial difference: this transformation tends to be temporary.

In the limbo between novels the detective figure undergoes a re-set back to how they were before, ready for the start of the next instalment in the meganarrative. In a crime fiction series each novel builds toward a perilous climax, which the protagonist survives, only for the process to be replicated in every subsequent instalment. Amnesia and the phoenix-like capacity to be reborn after every 'fire' are, I contend, integral to the construction of the crime series protagonist. Amnesia and rebirth are also direct evidence of the mythic template that ultimately curtails their trajectory. When considering the series by Rankin and Massey, there are indicators, as previously discussed, of the protagonists appearing to age and mature. The conventions of the series form can accommodate character development, but the detective figure's mythic and iterative qualities effectively constrain that potential such that the detective never seems to undergo a radical metamorphosis.

In formalist terms, the mythic hero emerges as a symbiotic byproduct of the series structure. But the crime series protagonist is also figured as mortal, with an ongoing life. The dichotomy between the two modes of representation is captured here by Eco, in his analysis of Superman, the 'mythological character of comic strips' (2005: 149):

> The mythic character embodies a law, or a universal demand, and therefore must be in part *predictable* and cannot hold surprises for us; the character of a novel wants, rather, to be a man like anyone else, and what could befall him is as unforeseeable as what may happen to us (148).

I argue that in contemporary crime series the protagonist effectively unifies the dichotomy expressed by Eco, creating a character that is 'mythic' but also 'like anyone else'. And it is Eco's ideas on a mythic character such as Superman, combined with Danielsson's position regarding the realism of contemporary detective figures, that I have taken as the foundations to my own theory of mythorealism.

A mythorealist reading can be applied to Child's Jack Reacher. On the mythic side, he presents as a powerful stranger who (repeatedly) saves the day. But study the meganarrative from a realist perspective, and the Reacher that emerges after twenty-four novels is: a vigilante responsible for killing, judge-and-jury style, countless opponents; a serial monogamist with a string of abandoned relationships; a figure whose fictional biography becomes impossible to chart. And yet Reacher is still treated as a realist figure. Child's series is not read or marketed as fantasy fiction. The Reacher series may be an outlier within the crime genre, but it points to how mythorealism shapes a character like Massey's Perveen Mistry, a protagonist equipped with an ongoing biography (relayed through references to her family, her taboo friendship with an Englishman, her growing ambitions as a lawyer), but who is destined to fulfil her role as a mythic hero, vanquishing the killer that all other 'mortals' have failed to apprehend. This same mythorealist pattern is also present in a series such as Rankin's. Rebus has a daughter, a number of relationships with women, a flat in Edinburgh, and an old Saab car, all details that make the character appear 'to be a man like anyone else'. But again, bringing an alternative reading to his meganarrative, what emerges is the heroic, activated, on-duty Rebus, the 'mythic character' who 'embodies a law, or a universal demand': a detective figure whose actions in the text are dictated by the generic conventions of the murder quest.

Within my definitions of mythorealism, Child's series displays the more mythic version of this theory, whereas in the series by Rankin and Massey there is more emphasis on the realism. In many ways, Child's series creates a world where, like that depicted in Golden Age fiction, society is 'fixed' and order reinstated when Reacher eradicates the guilty. In Rankin's series there is a different conception of criminality, and he argues that 'as readers, we … don't like superheroes … we like them to fail occasionally. And Rebus often feels that; he feels that maybe he got the right person for the wrong reason, or that solving a crime doesn't really make anything better' (2012: 72–3). Rankin defends the realism of Rebus by pointing to the protagonist's imperfections, his failures, and his helplessness in a world where 'solving a crime doesn't really make anything better'.

Relevant here is Abbott's research on white masculinity in Hardboiled fiction and film noir, and her observation that, 'These men repeatedly find themselves dissembling, fainting, unconscious, overpowered, and out of control while their ideals of masculinity continue to require of them self-discipline, toughness, and the quintessential hardness that gives the genre its name' (2002: 7). Although Abbott's ideas are directed at Hardboiled protagonists in 1930s–1950s American culture, a legacy of the friction between toughness/weakness and self-discipline/out-of-control is apparent in descendants of that tradition, such as Rebus. Another contemporary example of this conflicted character type is Texas Ranger Darren Matthews, the protagonist in Attica Locke's series. In the first chapter of #1 *Bluebird, Bluebird* Matthews is about to perjure himself to a grand jury:

> He wanted the jurors to get to know him, to be more inclined than not to believe he was telling the truth. He didn't trust that the badge would be enough, not looking the way he did now. The pits of his dress shirt were damp, and there was a rank funk seeping from his pores ... His stomach lurched, and he belched up something moist and sour (Locke, 2018: 16).

This is the fallen hero, steeped in his own rancid corporeality. The idea of the detective figure as fleshly and fallible has its roots in the Hardboiled era, but the argument I wish to emphasise is that in contemporary series the protagonist's flaws become a way of proving they are human and mortal: they feel things, they get injured, they struggle to do their job, they have sleepless nights. They are like you and me.

However, the apparent humanness of a character such as Rebus or Matthews can be disputed. Delve deeper, and their mythic tendencies are exposed. In many contemporary crime series the detective figure presents as seemingly realist, often very convincingly so, but it is a realism grafted onto a mythic template. And as will become clear in the next section, this fusion of myth and reality has at its core a conflict with gender.

4 Iconically Masculine?

In contemporary crime fiction series, the detective figure merges 'mythic hero' with 'real person'. This composite character is found in cosy series descended from Golden Age fiction, as well as in series deriving from the Hardboiled tradition. A cosy protagonist, such as Katherine Kovacic's Alex Clayton or Sujata Massey's Perveen Mistry, relies on intuition and deduction to solve a crime, whereas a neo-hardboiled character, such as Sara Paretsky's V.I. Warshawski or Ian Rankin's Inspector Rebus, uses physical force alongside cerebral methods. Regardless of apparent differences, I argue that across all subgenres the protagonist can be classed as mythorealist. In the following section, I examine how my theory intersects with gender: does the series form inevitably generate a mythic archetype that is male? In a study of feminism and the crime novel, Munt concludes:

> The image is archetypal – the warrior knight, the tough cowboy, the intrepid explorer – he is the representative of Man, and yet more than a man, he is the

focus of morality, the mythic hero ... Both the form and the content of this scenario are iconically masculine (2004: 1).

By populating these narratives with characters that embody 'mythic hero', the crime genre communicates an 'iconically masculine' message. This is evident in series featuring male and female protagonists, by male and female authors from across the globe, notably including: Leye Adenle, Sharon Bolton, Ann Cleeves, A.A. Dhand, Eva Dolan, Elizabeth George, Mari Hannah, Jane Harper, Oliver Harris, Keigo Higashino, Arnaldur Indridasson, Åsa Larsson, Adrian McKinty, Abir Mukherjee, Leonardo Padura, Louise Penny, Kathy Reichs, Emma Viskic, Roz Watkins, and Qiu Xiaolong. In this diverse range of series there is ample evidence of the argument presented by Plain, in her study on gender and sexuality in twentieth-century crime fiction: 'Whether the detective is male or female, straight or gay, she or he always exists in negotiation with a series of long-established masculine codes' (2001: 11). Masculinity also exerts an influence over non-binary protagonists, for example in Jack A. Ori's Cedarwood Campus series, where amateur detective C.J. Jennings adheres to the archetype of mythic hero in their pursuit of the murder quest. The crime series protagonist may be a woman, man, non-binary, queer, or straight, but they often transmit a masculinity codified as heroic, invincible, and autonomous: narrow definitions that fail to acknowledge that contemporary society embraces many different expressions of maleness. The way women are portrayed in crime fiction is also unrepresentative. When not cast as masculinised protagonist, the female characters typically take generic guises such as victim, femme fatale, mad woman, good girl, or sexualised corpse.

The crime genre has tended to promote a restrictive conception of gender. Looking ahead to future decades, when normative binaries further dissolve and gender identities continue to diversify, new words will supersede 'masculine' and 'feminine' in literary scholarship. Caldwell and Harris, in their recent study on quest design in video games, 'adopt a gender-neutral application of the term hero' (2024: 3); as an extension of this, a quest undertaken by an individual is described as 'singular', and a quest entailing collaboration is 'synergy', where the latter replaces (and de-genders) the concept of 'feminine-based models' (11). While acknowledging the potential of these alternative labels, in my own study I retain masculine and feminine, but with an important caveat: gender is performative and is understood within a trans-inclusive framework, where masculine and feminine define identity, not anatomy.

To illustrate how the crime genre's prevailing masculine codes are performed by a typical protagonist, I begin with an extract from Ian Rankin's series. In #17 *Exit Music*, Rebus is concerned 'some bespectacled penpusher' might defeat his arch nemesis: '[Rebus] wanted Cafferty taken out of the game. But suddenly it was important that it was *him* making the bone-crunching tackle' (2008: 268–9). Present here are the hallmarks of the masculinised protagonist: a hero acting in isolation, intent on 'making the bone-crunching tackle'. By giving Rebus attributes that reflect mainstream ideas of manhood in Western society, loner/driven/fighter, Rankin has created a character that readers will recognise as male. From #11 onward, Rankin brings in co-protagonist Detective Sergeant Siobhan Clarke as a counterpoint to Rebus: 'nice that she's female; you got a few sparks that fly between them' (2012: 80). But how do the genre's 'long-established masculine codes' impact on this female detective figure? Passages from Rankin's series show that male traits are indeed present in Clarke, for example, in #13 *Resurrection Men* when a sex worker is stabbed and Clarke grapples the male attacker: 'The knife again finding its target. Siobhan let go his arm and aimed her knee into his groin, connecting with all the force she could muster' (2001: 223). Clarke plays 'warrior knight' and the text signals how tough she is. This toughness is conveyed in masculine terms, through physical force, rather than via less gendered expressions of toughness, such as mental endurance. Rebus and Clarke exemplify how male mythic archetypes are incorporated in crime fiction series, but there are further ways in which masculinity has shaped character construction and the series form.

4.1 Gendering Work and Home and Time

Whether professional, semi-professional or amateur, the detective figure's 'job' is to solve a murder or major crime(s), and much of the narrative focuses on their on-duty hours, with few references to off-duty hours at home. Work has long been associated with masculinity, achievement, ambition, and independence, while the home is associated with femininity, nurturing, family, and community. These traditional interpretations are being challenged in contemporary society. In crime series, however, normative attitudes continue to shape the form, and the masculine presentation of character through work/quest often takes precedence over the feminine presentation of character through home/family/relationships. This is repeatedly apparent in Rankin's series and can be illustrated by two examples. Firstly, when Rebus contemplates his personal life in #17 *Exit Music*: 'Ciggies and booze and a little night music … he wondered if they would sustain him once the job was behind him. What else did he have? A daughter down in England, living with a college lecturer. An ex-wife who'd moved to Italy. The pub' (2008: 15). The estranging of Rebus from femininity and family is modelled in the physical distancing of his daughter and ex-wife. The gender-inflected privileging of work over personal life is also present in my second example, from #13 *Resurrection Men,* featuring Clarke, when a police counsellor asks:

> 'What about outside work? Are there any keen interests you have?'
> Siobhan thought for a long time. 'Music, chocolate, football, drink.' [...]
> 'Is there some sort of special relationship you're in just now?'
> 'Only with the job, Ms Thomson ... And I'm not absolutely sure it loves me any more'
>
> (Rankin, 2001: 439).

Clarke is 'married' to the job and her 'masculinity' is proclaimed via football and alcohol, inflected by a 'feminine' predilection for chocolate. To criticise Clarke as insufficiently feminine would be at odds with current nuanced perceptions of gender. Nevertheless, her character does demonstrate that in many series, such as Rankin's, the depictions of a personal life frequently reflect male archetypes.

Looking at how time is treated in these meganarratives, then gender once again has an impact. In series of longer duration, the detective figure's existence typically unfolds during the nebulous middle years. The protagonist may be around thirty in the first novel, and with each annually published instalment they proceed through the comparatively uniform years of middle age. Time moves on, according to the chronology of the novels, but it does not significantly alter the protagonist and, as shown in Section 3, an apparent amnesia shields them from the traumas of the job. The detective figure seems to mature, but old age is held at bay until it can no longer be ignored: for instance in the Rebus series when, after a lifetime of smoking, the character finally succumbs to a chronic health condition in #21. There is also, within the genre, minimal acknowledgement of how the biological clock might affect a female protagonist such as Rankin's Clarke, even though the later years of middle age equate to a loss of fertility.

I argue that the series form presents ageing as having no major repercussions because it tends to model a masculine conception of ageing. The principal way in which unchanging middle-ageness is maintained is through the distancing of family exemplified by Rankin's series. The masculinised hero-icised presentation of character is achieved by excising the feminised time-calibrated presence of progeny. Glenn Most summarised, in 1983, 'the basic generic conventions of the literary detective' (364), and although he failed to acknowledge the significance of gender, Most does allude to the avoidance of family and relationships: 'he is almost always single or divorced ... his parents are almost never mentioned, and he is invariably childless' (343).

If a detective figure has children, this places an onus on the author to pay more attention to recording the passage of time within the meganarrative, because children transform radically year by year. Remove procreation from the narrative and it allows the never-ageing of the protagonist to persist unchallenged. These observations tally with Eco's analysis of comic strips, where he highlights the chastity of mythic heroes by referencing Parsifal, a knight at King Arthur's round table: 'the "parsifalism" of Superman is one of the conditions that prevents his slowly "consuming" himself, and it protects him from the events, and therefore from the passing of time, connected with erotic ventures' (2005: 155).

The crime series protagonist is never consumed because their narrative arc is never concluded. At this point, I can bring further scrutiny to my concept of meganarrative. Crucially, I argue that it is an open-ended text. Along with the usual format of an ever-extending series with an instalment added each year, the crime genre also includes trilogies and quartets that appear to have a conclusion. However, there is scope to resume that limited series at a later date, via prequel or sequel instalments; even if the original series was terminated by the protagonist's death, a secondary character can potentially inherit the role. Nor is the author's retirement an obstacle, for example Lee Child's Jack Reacher series has, from #25 onward, been co-written with his brother Andrew. Meganarratives can also continue after an author's death, although these legacy series usually entail the resuscitation of old favourites from earlier eras, such as Sophie Hannah's continuation of Agatha Christie's Hercule Poirot series.

All of these instances reinforce my argument that the contemporary crime fiction series is an open-ended meganarrative supporting an open-ended character. The protagonist is never terminated and, extrapolating from Eco's theories on Superman, by persisting alone and childless the passing of time is less evident and the character is free to occupy 'a narrative plot which multiplies like a tapeworm; the greater its capacity to sustain itself through an indefinite series of contrasts, oppositions, crises, and solutions, the more vital it seems' (2005: 149). As an example of a tapeworm narrative Eco cites Alexandre Dumas's novels about the three musketeers, but his remarks are, I suggest, applicable to crime series. Across the meganarrative created by Rankin, John Rebus does have relationships with women, and a daughter from a failed marriage, but the Parsifalic model still applies, given that these factors never divert him from 'the oppositions, crises, and solutions' of the murder quest.

By effectively being shielded from procreation and a propulsive chronology, the overall timeframe of a typical crime series is able, and once again I draw on Eco's comments about Superman, to 'develop in a kind of oneiric climate – of which the reader is not aware at all – where what has happened before and what has happened after appear extremely hazy' (2005: 153). An evasive, dreamlike (oneiric) quality is maintained in Rankin's series by the absence of Rebus's daughter Samantha. She ages from child to adult across the series but features in just eight of the twenty-four novels, occasionally acquiring prominence. In #1 she is kidnapped, in #9 she is seriously injured, and in #23 she is suspected of murdering her partner. These are significant incidents, but I argue that Rebus having a daughter is only foregrounded in a few specific novels, and for most of the meganarrative her character is consigned to the background, allowing Rebus to be nebulously middle-aged (up until #21 when his health deteriorates).

This unshackling from time is also evident in Rebus's co-protagonist, Siobhan Clarke, whose Parsifalism is conspicuous. Danyté observes that Clarke 'seems asexual ... never having a steady boyfriend or even an occasional lover. Nor are there any references to earlier partners or sexual experiences' (2011: 47). Clarke does not have offspring, and although a character's gender need not be expressed through motherhood, it is worth noting that, by making her childless, Rankin evades one of the challenges a female protagonist might present to the genre. The potential 'threat' posed by family life has shaped other genres too, such as Westerns, Spindler remarking of Karl May's fiction that the prerequisite of a series protagonist is that their 'status quo must be preserved': 'A marriage would be an event that not only brings a (traditionally) irreversible change to the hero's life but also brings new responsibilities for the hero, making it more difficult for him to concentrate on his "calling"' (2013: 212, 213).

As exemplified by Rankin's series and the extracts cited earlier, the long-running convention in crime series of the detective figure as single/divorced/childless means the meganarrative can keep growing, and within each instalment 'what has happened before and what has happened after appear extremely hazy'. The text avoids an onerous personal life for the protagonist, allowing the murder investigation to be the primary focus. By reducing their existence to loner workaholic, this sidesteps any 'new responsibilities for the hero'. It also liberates the protagonist from time itself: their mortality is not measured against the ageing associated with fertility and children.

My findings in Sections 2 and 3 established that the series form generates a mythic archetype, with a detective figure designed and destined to pursue the quest. It is now evident, through further analyses of Rankin's series, that the 'ideal' way to serve those demands is to eliminate the feminine obstacles of family and a carnal chronology. Maintaining a fast pace within the prose, and keeping the plot directed at the murder, are hallmarks of the genre. These prerequisites encourage the removal of elements that might seem to slow or derail the narrative. This act of expediency tends to create a character that performs masculinity, but there are ways of challenging such a construct.

4.2 Disrupting Generic Conventions

In order to scrutinise gender and crime series character, it is necessary to step outside a genre whose conventions are so well established they often codify any attempts to apply a fresh perspective. Readers have been trained on texts where 'murder quest' and 'archetypal (masculine) hero' seem a natural fit. The series form suits the type of mythorealist character examined in Section 3, as the typical crime narrative only requires them to perform in a conventionally masculine and heroic way. Nevertheless there are series where these generic conventions are disrupted by femininity, for example, Sara Paretsky's V.I. Warshawski series:

> Showing a greater sensitivity to the needs of families, friends and children – and to the crimes that threaten them – has not compromised the contemporary female sleuth's toughness or gumption. In each of Sara Paretsky's novels, the irascible, but deeply loyal, Vic [Warshawski] winds up reluctantly seeking help from friends and neighbours (Kinsman, 2002: 162).

Warshawski's (masculine) 'toughness' is offset by a (feminine) 'sensitivity to the needs of families, friends and children'. Kinsman's study focuses on Paretsky's series along with Linda Barnes's Carlotta Carlyle series, which are taken to represent a list of female-authored/female-protagonist series, by Amanda Cross, Margaret Maron, Laurie King, Barbara Wilson, Kathleen V. Forrest, Barbara Neely, Valerie Wilson Wesley, Edna Buchanan, Joan Smith, Michelle Spring, Gillian Slovo, and Val McDermid (154). This group can be expanded to include Marcia Muller, Sue Grafton and other innovative authors writing in the 1970s, 80s, and 90s. Predominantly from the United States, these female authors have 'strategically redirected the masculinist trajectory of the American hard-boiled detective novel' toward feminist ends (Jones & Walton, 1999: 4). One such redirection has been situating the female protagonist in a community:

> This challenges the deeply embedded genre construct of the singular, abstract and judgemental code of the avenging knight (detective), answerable to no-one and set apart from his society.
>
> Instead, through the device of female friendship, the genre investigates one of our culture's abiding social constructs for females: the 'ethic of responsibility' ... the affiliative and co-operative connections with others which women are taught to value (Kinsman, 2002: 163, citing Gilligan).

I disagree with the position that these female series protagonists, embedded in a pseudo-family of friends, can challenge 'the singular, abstract and judgemental code of the avenging knight (detective)'. The loner workaholic simply becomes a sensitive loner workaholic with a few friends. Such friendship patterns still allow these female detectives to proceed with masculine autonomy. They have 'affiliative and co-operative connections with others', but typically the women protagonists are single, any children connected to them are likely to be a niece/nephew, and if there is a relationship with an older person, this will be a neighbour. Kinsman suggests that, 'Domestic arrangements of the detective and her friends, for example, may illustrate experiments in living other than the traditional nuclear family or the eccentric spinster model' (2002: 166). However, regardless of their 'experiments in living', I argue that the detectives in these series remain indebted to the Parsifalism highlighted by Eco (2005: 155).

These female protagonists are not always chaste but they are typically loners with no progeny, and thus conform to the (masculine) mythic hero. The character type created by feminist authors in the 1970s continues to be influential today and is apparent in Sujata Massey's series featuring lawyer Perveen Mistry. The protagonist has 'affiliative and co-operative connections' with her family and a female friend, and with the staff employed in her family's home and legal firm. Mistry also fits Eco's Parsifalic model: as established in #1, the laws of her religious community stipulate that Mistry can separate from but not divorce her abusive husband, therefore the protagonist is destined to remain single and childless. In subsequent novels Mistry has a close relationship with an Englishman, but they are restricted by religious custom and social taboos, and Mistry still complies with the Parsifalic masculine archetype.

As Denise Mina, author of several series, points out: 'Crime is a very hard genre to feminise' (2007). Mina has made her own bid to do this with series protagonist Detective Inspector Alex Morrow, but family/home rarely appear in the text and childcare is delegated to her husband. It is also worth noting that Mina's protagonist has an androgynous first name, and in many series the female lead has a name that masks her gender, such as Paretsky's Warshawski who is either V.I. or Vic. Mina goes on to say, 'If you have a female protagonist she is going to be looking after her mum when she gets older; she is going to be worried about her brother and sister; she will be making a living while bringing up kids' (2007). Mina indicates the norms that frame womanhood in contemporary society, but she ascribes these caring roles as only relevant to a female protagonist.

My examination of how to disrupt generic conventions has, so far, considered various initiatives to feminise crime fiction. I have also looked at how such initiatives are reflected in series by more recent authors, including Sujata Massey and Denise Mina. Female authors have undoubtedly brought major changes to the form, with their revisionist reappropriation of the traditional detective figure, but their protagonists still exhibit the markers of those pre-existing masculine conventions.

However, a key point remains to be made. When Danielsson identified the shift toward a life-story structure in contemporary crime series, she attributed this to societal factors: 'Private lives have become public concerns, not only in detective fiction but also in every arena from culture to politics' (2003: 10). I contend that this impetus to narrate the protagonist's personal life comes from inside the crime genre. Here is the real revolution brought about by the feminist authors mentioned earlier. It was female authors writing female-led crime series who engineered this change by responding to feedback from readers. When Maxine O'Callaghan, author of the Delilah West series, was interviewed in 1995 she stated: 'Today's series is really an ongoing story about the character's life. And believe me, readers want that. The comments I get from fans are about what's happening to Delilah personally, not often about plot' (quoted in Jones & Walton, 1999: 153). By situating their detective figures within a network of friends and familial relationships, and carrying that group forward from novel to novel, these pioneering female authors created the biographic impulse that has transformed the genre.

4.3 Performing Femininity

Feminist authors have had a major impact on the crime fiction series, but the examples cited so far still show the presence of masculine mythic archetypes. I now turn to another innovative author, Liza Marklund, for evidence of a more radical challenge to the 'iconically masculine' conventions of the series form. First published in 1998, her neo-hardboiled series is set in Sweden and there are eleven novels, with the works referenced here translated into English by Neil Smith. Protagonist Annika Bengtzon is an investigative journalist on the crime desk of a Swedish national paper and she fits my definition of semi-professional detective. Her role meets genre expectations, but the character also has a husband along with caring responsibilities for their children. Plain states that 'the provision of a stable relationship' constitutes 'a familiar generic rock' on which authors may founder: 'the same rock that has troubled writers from the "golden age" on. If the detective is to be the archetypal loner, then lovers must remain disposable' (2001: 185). Bengtzon defies that archetype as she has a husband, a family, and Bergman also notes, 'While the American women detectives tend to create their own "chosen families" of friends ... Bengtzon seeks to create her belonging primarily in the shape of a nuclear family' (2015: 117, citing Reddy).

There are undoubted similarities between the Bengtzon series and those written at an earlier date by the feminist authors listed by Kinsman (2002: 154). Marklund describes Bengtzon as 'limitless and a lone ranger' (2011a), and her protagonist still partially adheres to the genre's masculine mythic codes. In

Last Will her home is firebombed, and, after rescuing her children using 'superhuman' strength, Bengtzon jumps from an upper window 'just as the room behind her exploded into a firestorm' (2012: 506). The protagonist is modelled here as brave, strong, fearless, and Bergman observes that 'the end of the novel sees a Bengtzon who is true to the archetypal hardboiled hero: after repeated blows she still manages to save the day' (2015: 118).

However, what Marklund does is add further pressure to her detective figure by increasing the emphasis on family. Bengtzon is a 'lone ranger' but the author includes children when describing her protagonist: 'she wants a career and her kids' (2011a). Bengtzon's portrayal as both hero and mother makes her a subversive figure in the genre. The issue is not the 'unusualness' of Bengtzon having a family, but how much attention Marklund devotes to this. In my earlier analysis of Rankin's Inspector Rebus series, I showed that Siobhan Clarke's minimal off-duty life comprises 'Music, chocolate, football, drink' (Rankin, 2001: 439). By contrast, Marklund offers a detailed depiction of Bengtzon during non-working hours:

> She'd just laid the table and lit the candles when Thomas got home . . . 'I think I'm halfway there,' he said, giving Annika a quick kiss on the hair. 'This job's made for me. My CV is perfect, and with my personal contacts in the department, I can't see how anyone could beat me to it. Haven't you made any salad? . . . I thought we'd agreed to have something green with every meal,' he said, turning towards her.
>
> 'We did,' Annika said. My day's been absolutely great as well, she thought. I've been out to the Karolinska Institute and talked to a murder victim's work colleague. The police are about to arrest a group of German terrorists and I went shopping and made dinner. Aloud, she said: 'Can you get the kids while I chop up some salad?' She went to the fridge with a lump in her throat (2012: 90–1).

The protagonist is shown struggling to maintain a household, feed a family, and do a full-time job, namely, those aspects that Mina suggested were incompatible with the genre (2007). The feminine-inflected elements of family/home/relationships are given prominence in Marklund's female-led series. This becomes clear when comparing the Bengtzon and Rebus series, via representative novels: scenes featuring Bengtzon at home comprise 25 per cent of *Last Will* (Marklund, 2012), whereas only 10 per cent of the text depicts Rebus and Clarke at home in *Resurrection Men* (Rankin, 2001).

The content of these home scenes can be further analysed. In Rankin's series they are mostly linked to the murder investigation, for example, Rebus and Clarke discussing the case in his or her flat. The home scenes in Marklund's series also have content related to Bengtzon's enquiries, such as phone calls to police contacts, but the majority is generated by Bengtzon's relationships with her husband and children. In addition to a quarter of the novel being spent in Bengtzon's home, a further proportion is devoted to personal-life scenes elsewhere, with trips to the children's nursery/pre-school, a party at her parents-in-law, a visit to her friend's flat. *Resurrection Men* also has a few scenes outside the home that show Rebus's relationship with his current girlfriend, but they are confined to a few pages.

In most contemporary crime series, and here I reference Russian Formalism, the protagonist's downtime, and their 'life' between novels, is elided as the forgettable *fabula* of daily existence, leaving the *syuzhet* to be constructed from the criminal investigation (where fabula applies to the chronological sequence of events that provide material for a novel, and syuzhet applies to how that material is edited and reordered). In Rankin's series, the syuzhet focuses on Rebus's job as Detective Inspector, indeed the character 'needs' that role: 'Subtract work from the equation and the day became flabby, like releasing jelly from its mould' (Rankin, 2003: 79). Rebus's personal life is 'flabby' as there is no spouse/family giving it structure. A set of priorities is enacted in the prose. The domestic aspects of existence have traditionally been 'women's work' and crime fiction has always tended to reflect a patriarchal dismissal of home life, by directing the syuzhet primarily at the murder quest.

However, in Marklund's series, Bengtzon's personal life is narrated alongside the murder quest. The syuzhet is constructed from two interweaving strands: the job Bengtzon does at home, maintaining a family (the personal narrative), and the job she does in the workplace, as an investigative journalist (the murder narrative). This dualling signals that both roles are significant. Marklund challenges the androcentric conventions of the genre. When considering the traditional gendering of home and work, it could be argued that Bengtzon performs femininity in her personal life and performs masculinity as an investigative journalist. Such an interpretation is fundamentally flawed. I contend that where Bengtzon performs femininity is in the way the character balances her domestic and professional commitments. Regardless of whether we are female/male/non-binary, I argue that 'performing femininity' is what most of us do every day, to varying degrees, but this quotidian negotiation between domestic/professional and private/public is rarely seen in crime narratives.

Relating to actions and behaviour, not anatomy, it is this holistic understanding of existence that is portrayed in the character type I define as the feminised protagonist. The majority of crime series have a masculinised protagonist, the archetype of mythic hero, devoid of a functioning home life, but the series form also accommodates a detective figure who performs femininity. This may not involve a nuclear family, as evident in the series by Barbara Neely and Walter

Mosley. The key point is that the feminised protagonist has personal obligations toward other characters, likely to include some of these: spouse/partner, children, relatives, friends, colleagues, and local community. A feminised protagonist such as Liza Marklund's Annika Bengtzon has affinities with Sara Paretsky's V.I. Warshawski. There are also similarities with a character like Sujata Massey's Perveen Mistry, in terms of the increased focus on personal life within the narrative.

However, what distinguishes a feminised protagonist is how they present the complexity of existence, where the detective figure struggles to reconcile the conflicting demands of the murder quest and their onerous personal responsibilities. Eco states that for a series to keep on growing, instalment after instalment, the protagonist has to be protected 'from the events, and therefore from the passing of time, connected with erotic ventures' (2005: 155). Across the meganarrative arc, Marklund's Bengtzon marries, has two children, divorces, marries again, becomes stepmother to two further children, and, by the end of the final novel, has adopted her niece and is pregnant. Bengtzon defies the Parsifalic model: contrary to Eco's position, Marklund's series has still been able to sustain itself through eleven murder quests. Eco's theories shed light on crime series but they only define the masculine variation of the form, where ageing and family/relationships are effectively diminished. When domestic considerations and a carnal chronology are incorporated in the narrative, this fully developed personal life gives rise to a feminine variation.

I posed the question earlier: does the series form inevitably produce a mythic archetype that is male? It is my contention that the contemporary form also creates a mythic archetype that is female, and in the next section, I study this figure in detail and consider the influence of feminisation on the genre.

5 Character in Extremis

In the contemporary crime fiction series, the character-shaping tendencies typically generate a masculinised detective figure, but the form's conventions also accommodate a feminised figure; this variation has emerged as a result of the increased focus on personal life and the biographic arc. The female archetype has a more developed home life and the series often shows the protagonist striving to fulfil personal/domestic commitments alongside conducting an investigation. This section considers how feminisation affects the definition of mythorealism established in Section 3. I also examine how my theory can adapt to the many different detective figures that populate the genre nowadays, from overtly mythic to highly realist.

To demonstrate the impact of feminisation on character construction, I begin with the techniques used to incorporate a personal narrative in novels traditionally focused on the murder quest. In a typical series like Ian Rankin's Inspector Rebus, with its masculinised protagonist, the personal scenes tend to be intermittent. One such scene, in #13 *Resurrection Men,* features Rebus taking a trip with his current girlfriend: 'They left the curtains and the window open, so that the first thing they'd see on waking would be Loch Etive. Then they fell asleep in one another's arms. Sunday, they didn't rise till nine, blaming the country air as they embraced and kissed' (375). This passage differs from the rest of the narrative: elements of romantic fiction have been inserted in a crime novel. Rebus also appears to have shed the core traits of contrarian, brooding, and pessimist, discussed in Section 2.

Personal scenes have the potential to cause inconsistencies in genre and characterisation. It is not a concern in Rankin's series because his personal life occupies a small proportion of the novels. However, series with a feminised protagonist have numerous personal scenes: does this increase the risk of slippages? Taking as my example Liza Marklund's series, with investigative journalist Annika Bengtzon, there is no evidence of this and the protagonist's traits remain consistent. Bengtzon is not 'a different person' at home, and we see her being tormented, obsessive, and volatile, in the personal narrative and in the murder narrative. Occasionally the protagonist is shown enjoying family life, playing with her children (2011b: 295), but often the novels feature arguments, such as in *Last Will* when Bengtzon's husband discovers she knows about his extra-marital relationship:

> '*Stop lying to me!*' he shouted, grabbing her shoulder and spinning her round so fast she almost fell.
> 'Ow,' she said, looking up at his face, all red and distorted.
> 'How long have you been *pretending?*' he yelled. 'How the hell could you *do* this to me?'
> She felt anger explode in her gut with such force that she could hardly breathe. '*Me?*' she said. 'How could *I* do this to *you*? Are you mad, you fucking disgusting unfaithful *bastard?*'
> (Marklund, 2012: 476).

Their encounter is full of tension and conflict, as are many of the scenes about Bengtzon's home life. The personal narrative has moments of mystery, violence, and suspense: it exhibits the same genre-defining elements found in the murder narrative. This, I suggest, is the technique that enables personal-life scenes to be integrated into the novel while maintaining consistency of characterisation and genre.

My concept of the feminised protagonist is also applicable to male detective figures, exemplified by Walter Mosley's series. Easy Rawlins, a private investigator, is portrayed as devoted to his two adopted children, orphaned by the crimes in #1 and #3, and the series demonstrates that a feminised protagonist is not limited to the traditional family depicted in Marklund's novels. Mosley's series contains many passages where Rawlins is maintaining a home life for his children alongside pursuing enquiries. A parallel can be drawn with Ruth Rendell's Inspector Reginald Wexford series, a police procedural set in the United Kingdom. Stoddard Holmes points out, 'the fact that [Wexford] has a traditional home life, complete with spouse, children and grandchildren, distinguishes him among detectives' (1997: 151): a salient reminder that masculinised protagonists tend to dominate the genre. However, comparing Wexford to Rawlins, the recurring family characters in Rendell's series are less developed, and Wexford's wife Dora is 'neither objectified nor given a subjectivity' (155). Supplying the protagonist with a family/elderly relative but downplaying their presence in the text is apparent in other series such as Denise Mina's Inspector Morrow, discussed earlier, as well as Ann Cleeves's Inspector Perez, and Elizabeth George's Inspector Lynley and Barbara Havers. Along with Rendell's Wexford, they indicate that a detective with a personal life is not necessarily a feminised protagonist: it is the treatment of this personal life, exemplified by Mosley's Rawlins and Marklund's Bengtzon, that is the key factor.

Analysing the additional conventions of a feminised protagonist, it is evident that the dualling of the personal and murder narratives, discussed in Section 4, becomes a means of emphasising an author's themes. Marklund shows Bengtzon struggling to meet societal expectations of motherhood and also combatting sexism in a male-dominated workplace (2012: 90–1, 2011b: 45–7). The author highlights her feminist message about the difficulties women encounter when trying to balance home and career. Bergman suggests Marklund's model is more common in Sweden (2014: 83), and Hill notes that many Nordic female authors concentrate on 'the personal lives of their protagonists, so that the crime element of the book, although remaining significant to the narrative, is not always the main focus' (2017: 276).

A particular method is used to transmit these political/thematic concerns, via the narration of the feminised protagonist, but I begin by considering a more typical series, such as Rankin's. Here, the personal scenes often relate to the murder investigation, for example, in #13 *Resurrection Men* when a police colleague visits Siobhan Clarke for coffee in her flat: this is ostensibly a social call but, in a narratologically expedient fashion, Clarke learns new information that helps with her enquiry into crime boss Cafferty (2001: 70–4). In Marklund's series, on the other hand, there are storylines in Bengtzon's personal life that are unconnected to her role as investigative journalist. In *Last Will* Bengtzon's son is injured and she confronts the boys responsible: 'If you are ever mean to Kalle again, and I mean *ever*, I'll kill you' (Marklund, 2012: 440). This scene has no direct bearing on the murder quest: its significance lies in how it augments the themes of *Last Will*. Bengtzon threatens to kill a child in a novel where she is investigating a female assassin, thereby exposing society's gendered attitudes: female violence is typically judged as more transgressive than male violence. Throughout the series, Marklund creates parallels between the personal and murder narratives, and my term for this is 'mirroring'.

Mirroring is also present in Barbara Neely's Blanche White series, set in the United States, and first published in 1992. Neely signals race as a central concern through double naming a black character as white, and the four novels are a crossover between the neo-hardboiled/cosy subgenres. White is a single parent who has adopted her niece and nephew, offering another example of a feminised protagonist with a non-traditional family. The series usually shows White operating as amateur detective while working as housekeeper to privileged white families. However, in #2 *Blanche Among the Talented Tenth* White is holidaying at an exclusive resort, built by a black entrepreneur who made his fortune from skin-lightening and hair-straightening products; the wealthy African Americans who stay there are predominantly light-skinned (2020: loc. 2948, 2915). The protagonist investigates a suspicious death and a suicide, and Neely uses the narrative to explore ideas of the authentic self. In the murder narrative, White uncovers the true nature of various characters, including Robert Stuart, a local pharmacist: he fostered the misunderstanding that caused the suicide (loc. 6208). White also investigates his past: Stuart is black, and after his Asian wife died, he dumped her body 'like she was a bag of trash', because his father would disown him for marrying 'outside the race' (loc. 6187, 6177). At the start of the novel, these deceptions are not apparent, and Stuart becomes White's lover. But when her enquires threaten to expose him, he viciously attacks her, and White states: 'Everything about him looked phony to her now' (loc. 5263, 6208).

These themes are then augmented by Neely in the personal narrative. White is proud of her 'deep-black skin' and 'hair in its natural state' (loc. 2882, 3771), but her niece Taifa wants White to straighten her hair before arriving at the resort and is concerned about her own skin darkening in the sun (loc. 2992, 4171). White and Taifa are shown to have different ideas about authentic self-expression, though White recognises that skin colour does not define her identity: 'She could picture herself a hundred shades lighter ... but she couldn't make the leap to wanting to step out of the talk, walk, music, food, and feeling of being black' (loc. 3166). The deaths in *Blanche Among the Talented Tenth* are associated with people concealing who they 'truly' are, and Neely uses mirroring between the murder narrative and White's personal narrative to emphasise that wider societal pressures and prejudices are often the reason why an individual might be corrupted.

Through my analyses I have added to the concept of the feminised detective figure. Danielsson's observation that the crime fiction series has become 'a life story in installments' (2003: 1) did not tally with my earlier findings on Rankin's Rebus series, where that life story was limited. But the series by Marklund, Neely, and Mosley appear a closer match, indeed Danielsson cites Mosley's Easy Rawlins to illustrate her argument (2002: 94–103). These three series may seem to diverge from mythorealism, with characters that are so realist as to lose their mythic underpinnings. However, as seen in Section 4, Marklund's Bengtzon still behaves like a mythic hero, for example, when her home explodes (2012: 506), and there are multiple instances in Mosley's series of Rawlins's superhuman/mythic tendencies, such as the finale of #12 *Little Green*: 'I strained against my would-be killer with a primordial effort' (2014: 284).

I now bring further scrutiny to the gendering of myth as expressed through the series form. In Campbell's theory of monomyth (1973), discussed in Section 3, quest is conceived as conquest: this reflects masculine archetypes via a hero's journey that is external. However, Hudson proposes, in counterpoint to Campbell, the feminine archetypes present in fairy tales. These stories often take place in the domestic realm, and the character's journey is an internal one toward 'psychological independence' (2010: 7). This same inner quest is found in series featuring a feminised detective figure. In Neely's #2 *Blanche Among the Talented Tenth*, White contemplates her journey toward wellbeing: 'Since she'd begun her spiritual practice, she felt more firmly rooted in, not on, the ground' (loc. 3802). Similarly, in Mosley's #13 *Rose Gold*, Rawlins's final words are an assessment of his emotional trajectory: 'Maybe it's time I learn to count my blessings' (2015: 308).

Based on the series by Marklund, Neely, and Mosley, there is evidence that the outer conquest of the traditional crime series has been merged with an inner quest for self-knowledge, and the feminised protagonist combines aspects inherited from masculine as well as feminine archetypes in myths and fairy tales. However, this inner journey is only narrated when a murder has occurred, initiating the novel. Earlier, I proposed that the contemporary crime series is a record of the detective figure's involvement in criminal investigations, and that huge portions of their lives are omitted. To this I add the contingent point that, regardless of whether they are feminised or masculinised, these characters only get to narrate their personal lives when they also have a crime to solve.

When considering the murder narrative, there are indicators here too of gender having an effect, particularly on the autonomy of the detective. In a typical series, this autonomy, as noted by Most, is often expressed through the detective being single, divorced, childless, and parentless (1983: 343). He then states, 'It is his freedom from all such categories that permits him so clearly to see through their workings in all the other characters' (343). Rankin's series exemplifies this, with its masculinised protagonists. Rebus is depicted in on-off relationships, Clarke is perpetually single, and both of them are shown to have autonomy, freed as they are from the personal obligations that often complicate the lives of the characters they investigate in the novels. Rebus and Clarke's autonomy is further reinforced through their position as publicly appointed police detectives, a role that requires them to stand apart from the community, to surveil people, and make judgements on the legality of their actions.

For a feminised protagonist like Marklund's Bengtzon, her autonomy is more conflicted, and again I draw parallels with mythology. Frankel argues against Campbell, identifying what she terms 'the heroine's journey' in myths and fairy tales, which feature a female protagonist and her 'struggle for autonomy' (2010: 8). This struggle is evident in Bengtzon, who is shown to cherish her freedom from family obligations: 'When the nursery door closed behind her she always felt a huge sense of relief. Hours of unbroken concentration lay ahead and she could take possession of her brain until a quarter to four' (2012: 125). This highlights the gendered nature of autonomy and Bergman notes, 'Throughout the series Bengtzon fluctuates between the roles of "conflicted mother" and "lone avenger"' (2015: 112). Marklund also reworks the genre's positioning of the detective figure as source of authority. In *Exposed*, chronologically the first of the series, Bengtzon is abused by her boyfriend and subjected to coercive control and repeated assaults; she murders him and is convicted of manslaughter. This traumatic backstory is recalled by Bengtzon in subsequent novels. By presenting Bengtzon as a woman who has survived domestic violence and killed her abuser, Marklund dismantles 'the deeply embedded genre construct of the singular, abstract and judgemental code of the avenging knight (detective), answerable to no-one and set apart from his society' (Kinsman, 2002: 163).

Not only is Bengtzon's autonomy affected by gender, her position as the figure of authority is destabilised in the novels; the protagonist 'policing' the criminals is herself a convicted criminal. Victimhood is part of Bengtzon's characterisation, and an unchosen victimhood is also present in Easy Rawlins. Mosley's series has many passages detailing the difficulties the protagonist faces as an African American trying to raise a family and earn money in a society rife with prejudice. Rawlins's authority as 'the detective' is frequently challenged when speaking to the white populace of Los Angeles. That same challenge shapes his dealings with the city's predominantly white police service, even when, in #9 *Little Scarlet*, Rawlins is employed by them to investigate a murder during the 1965 riots:

> The cops coming at us numbered four. They were all white men. They all had their pistols drawn.
> In my left hand I held the letter given to me by [Deputy Commissioner] Gerald Gordon.
> 'Before you make a mistake, officers,' I said. 'Please read this letter.'
> I hadn't been pistol whipped for some time.
> The advanced policeman struck me for no reason I could see (Mosley, 2005: 100).

Rawlins is investigating a murder but he is shown to question the power structures that impede his existence. He is violently assaulted 'for no reason I could see', though there are clear indications here and elsewhere that racism is the reason. In crime fiction 'the ultimate subject is the society in which such murders are performed' (Most, 1983: 365): Marklund, Neely, and Mosley demonstrate how this scrutiny can be reinforced through the narration of the protagonist's lived experience. Structural inequalities are often what has instigated the murder featured in their novels, but these same inequalities constrain the feminised detective figure. The murder victim is a victim, but so is the detective.

In conservative interpretations of the series form, the novels suggest that incarcerating criminals can 'cure' society and restore order. Marklund, Neely, and Mosley are seen to question this, along with lots of other authors who, via differing approaches, have extended the scope of the teleologically oriented murder quest. In these more ambitious series, examples of which increased in frequency from the 1930s onward, 'blame' is directed at sociopolitical factors, where the wider community is shown to be culpable, rather than the individual. The genre is broad as well as versatile. Particularly in the current era, it contains a vast array of different series, each with a distinctive protagonist. But regardless of this diversity, I argue that a single theory unites these many variations on the detective figure found in the contemporary series form.

5.1 Mythorealist Spectrum

I have already established that, in a contemporary crime fiction series, the detective figure is mythorealist. The conventions of mythorealism tend to produce a masculinised protagonist, but these same conventions also encompass a feminised protagonist. Returning to my definition in Section 3, the theory can now be expanded and unified: I propose that mythorealism is a spectrum. At the mythic end are the more masculinised detective figures, and at the realist end are the more feminised detective figures. A number of series have been examined in this Element, and to illustrate my argument I have situated these on the mythorealist spectrum, showing the range of detective figures being created by contemporary authors:

- protagonists that display an extreme mythicism (Lee Child's Jack Reacher)
- protagonists that incorporate more realism but are still underlyingly mythic (Ian Rankin's John Rebus and Siobhan Clarke, Sara Paretsky's V.I. Warshawski, Katherine Kovacic's Alex Clayton, Attica Locke's Darren Matthews, and P.D. James's Adam Dalgliesh)
- protagonists where the mythic is further suppressed and the realism increased (Sujata Massey's Perveen Mistry and Ruth Rendell's Reginald Wexford)
- protagonists where realism is at the forefront (Liza Marklund's Annika Bengtzon, Barbara Neely's Blanche White, and Walter Mosley's Easy Rawlins)

When these character types are compared to my findings on gender, the first three categories equate to behaviours associated with masculinity, whereas the more realist figures display feminine patterns. Every author creates their own unique series character, but I contend that each protagonist is situated on this spectrum: from the masculinised and more overtly mythic, to the feminised and more overtly realist. These multiple expressions of the detective figure are available to female and male protagonists and also embrace non-binary as well as trans identities. Through my concept of the mythorealist spectrum I critically rework and update Eco and Danielsson.

However, there is a further question to consider: are there attributes that unite all these seemingly different protagonists? If I begin at the realist end of the spectrum, many of the genre's codes hold true for a detective figure such as Marklund's Bengtzon, indicating that she has been constructed by inflecting rather than rejecting the conventions outlined in Sections 2 and 3. Bengtzon's realism does not supplant her mythic/heroic qualities, and her victimhood complicates but does not usurp her position as an autonomous source of authority; the protagonist still operates as 'detective', even though the legitimacy of her role is disputed by other figures in the text.

Crime fiction tends to promote a restrictive conception of gender, and a compromised conception of race. Thanks to innovative series by authors such as Marklund, Neely, and Mosley, the relationships with prejudice are being rewritten. There are also authors seeking to challenge (mis)representations of non-normative sexuality and (mis)representations of persons with a disability or who are neurodiverse, in a genre that has traditionally equated 'difference' with criminality. Even in more progressive examples of the contemporary crime fiction series certain conventions persist, which unify this hugely varied and at times divergent genre, from cosy to neo-hardboiled, from the traditional to the experimental.

When seeking to identify the genre-defining constituents of the mythorealist protagonist, what emerges is a compulsive truth-seeker. This obsession sets them apart from 'the average person', creating a detective figure condemned to be a misfit, a loner. In Child's Reacher series as well as Rankin's Rebus series, this loner status is physical; they are excluded from conventional domesticity, and Rebus confesses to a colleague, 'This job's taken away my wife, my kid ... most of the friends I ever had' (2001: 191). By comparison, Marklund's Bengtzon is embedded in a family, and yet she alternates 'between striving for belonging and being a loner – sometimes even an outcast' (Bergman, 2015: 120). In Bengtzon's case, her loner status is emotional rather than physical: 'Who am I? ... Is there something destructive within me that I can't control?' (Marklund, 2012: 500–1). Bengtzon is shown as compelled to do her job as a journalist, and these same obsessive qualities are present in Rebus: 'He thought about the job too much as it was, gave himself to it the way he had never given himself to any *person* in his life' (Rankin, 2011c: 93).

The crime series protagonist may be female/male/non-binary, or masculinised/feminised in their performance, but isolation and compulsion are the two fundamental traits that equip them to pursue the murder quest. It is the detective figure's status as an outcast, their inability to 'fit in', their inner and outer unease, and their restlessness, which drives them to seek answers outside themself that they cannot find within. The detective strives for absolution and resolution, but these will always be withheld by the unfolding of the series form, which confronts them with yet another murder, yet another crisis, and yet another do-or-die situation.

Here the argument can be brought back to formalist terms. In literature, one of the methods used to give a character lead status is through segregating them from others in the text. This tactic is pushed to its limits in crime series. The detective figure, so carefully signalled as a loner, is the literary manifestation of attention-seeking subjectivity, and the murder quest turns them into a vehicle for narrative compulsion. The crime series protagonist is the inescapable outcome when you take the customary tools of literature and extend them ad infinitum and in extremis, intensifying all those character-producing techniques such as difference, isolation, compulsion, arc, and progression.

In ending Section 5, I wish to cast off notions of masculine and feminine, as these are masking a deeper understanding. When gender is stripped away, what you are left with is the perpetual loner on a perpetual mission. The detective in crime series is the supreme embodiment of what literature does when it generates character. There is no respite for this figure. The narrative will not let them settle. The crime series protagonist can never, ever, come in from the cold.

6 'An Underappreciated Revolution in Storytelling'

Edgar Allan Poe is often cited as the inventor of detective fiction. With the publication in 1841 of his short story, 'The Murders in the Rue Morgue', the author created the figure of Auguste Dupin, who became a model for subsequent fictional detectives. When Poe published two further stories featuring Dupin, he in effect invented the crime fiction series, and the potential of this new form was exploited by authors such as Arthur Conan Doyle, Catherine Louisa Pirkis, and John Edward Bruce. These innovations were happening alongside developments in other genres, and Strong points to a broad trend that has emerged in the past two hundred years: 'the widespread adoption of recurring characters in the novel and the subsequent, accelerating, embrace of this device across the newer media of cinema, radio, television and the web ... has amounted to an underappreciated revolution in storytelling' (2020: 110). This transformation in storytelling has impacted on the crime genre, both in terms of numerous series featuring recurring characters, and the many adaptations into other media.

At the heart of the contemporary crime fiction series is a figure who 'detects', who gathers and interprets clues, who solves mysteries and catches killers. However, the word 'detective' was not used by Poe to describe his amateur sleuth Dupin. The term first appears in an 1843 article on 'The London Police' in *Chambers's Edinburgh Journal*, where it was reported that 'Intelligent men have been recently selected to form a body called the "detective police", intended to solve more complex crimes' (Chambers & Chambers: 54). The rank of detective has, since the 1840s, been part of police forces worldwide, but alongside this publicly appointed investigator there has emerged an entrepreneurial figure: in different countries and eras this individual has been known as a private investigator or P.I., a private eye, a gumshoe, a private dick, a sleuth, a shamus, and they meet the needs of those seeking a more personal service. These early beginnings of 'the detective', in the police, the private sector, and Poe's fiction, together constitute the origins of the literary character that has come to dominate the crime genre.

Throughout my study I have often referred to the lead character in crime series as 'the protagonist', to reflect that the investigative figure in contemporary series may be far removed from traditional notions of a detective. The genre still has series featuring police detectives and P.I.'s, but nowadays it also includes protagonists that utilise the transferrable skills from their role as a lawyer, forensic pathologist, journalist, and other comparable professions, along with protagonists where the link seems more tenuous, such as a priest, tea shop owner, university professor, gardener, and so on. Such figures have extended the scope of crime fiction, but regardless of the content of these series, the lead character is focused on investigating a murder or major crime(s).

This Element is a record of my life-long love affair with the detective figure. My aim has been to establish the primacy of character as a generative force within the contemporary crime fiction series. By examining how the protagonist is created and maintained, I have revealed many of the conventions that underpin these modern meganarratives. My study has critically reworked current scholarship by identifying that mythorealism is the theory that defines the contemporary detective figure. I have also shown that the crime fiction series can engage with fundamental ideas about human existence, as well as different conceptions of gender and identity. But the crime genre and the series form are continuing to evolve, and Section 6 looks ahead to future trends.

6.1 Future Trends

Since the beginning of the genre, certain qualities have been apparent in the crime fiction series, but there is no fixed formula and there never has been. To call these fictions formulaic is to miss the experimentation, the evolution, the playfulness. I now turn my attention to a number of ground-breaking series and predict new developments.

All my discussions so far have been about human protagonists, but the genre offers scope for 'setting' as a character. Crime series often feature a particular city or region, and, as the series unfolds, that place operates as a 'living' character alongside the detective figure (Latimer, 2021a). Sloma points to this in Ian Rankin's series: 'in Edinburgh, Rankin has created such a real, active setting that it has become a character, and it develops just as much as, if not more than, John Rebus' (2012: 53). The significance of place within the crime genre can be traced to its antecedents in the gothic tradition, a literature where, as noted by Durot-Boucé, 'Haunted or haunting, architectural or vegetal . . . the setting is of major importance, becoming as much a protagonist of the story as the characters themselves' (210). When considering future trends in crime series, I foresee setting being reconfigured via a concept I term 'multisubjectival place', embracing a living environment that merges land, time, geology, weather, building, waterscape, vegetation, and all creatures, human or otherwise. Here I affiliate myself with actor-network theory as interpreted via Felski: 'Rejecting the divisions of subject/object, nature/culture, thought/matter, and language/world, [Bruno] Latour's work presumes the equal ontological salience of all classes of being in a mutually composed world' (2015: 738).

These alternative ways of conceiving 'place' and notions of character and subjectivity are apparent in Tana French's Dublin Murder Squad series, a police procedural set in contemporary Ireland, first published in 2007. Each of the six novels features a different Garda detective as protagonist, making it unusual in the genre, but the innovation I wish to highlight is how French explores multi-subjectivity in her treatment of setting, for example, in #4 *Broken Harbour* when Detective Kennedy enters the crime scene in a family's home and sees the view outside: 'the sea, high today, raising itself up at me green and muscled' (23). The author treats place as protagonist but also antagonist: the 'broken' house in the novel precipitates three murders; the location itself, Broken Harbour, also exerts a malevolent influence, scene as it was of Kennedy's mother's suicide during a family holiday. French's novel depicts the setting as somewhere that is animate, apparent in this description of a journey: 'The haunted blackness of the estate, scaffolding bones looming up out of nowhere, stark against the stars; then the smooth speed of the motorway, cat's-eyes flicking in and out of existence and the moon keeping pace off to one side, huge and watchful' (201).

Another novel that explores the literary potential of place as multisubjectival and teeming with life is Jon McGregor's *Reservoir 13* (2018). This sits on the edge of the genre, but it is a harbinger of future developments. The novel has aspects of nature writing, but it does concern the unsolved disappearance of teenager Rebecca Shaw who goes missing during a family holiday in Derbyshire. The narrative follows the rural community and the place itself in the thirteen years after that event. This shortened extract gives a sense of how different it is to a traditional crime novel:

> In the beech wood the foxes gave birth, earthed down in the dark and wet with pain, the blind cubs pressing against their mothers for warmth ... The reservoirs were a gleaming silver-grey, scuffed by the wind and lapping against the breakwater shores ... a man by the side of the road, his arm held out as though asking for help. He wasn't wearing the charcoal-grey coat but it looked like the missing girl's father ... At the parish council there were more apologies recorded than there were people in the room ... There were hard winds in the evenings and the streetlights shook in the square (35).

The prose has an even, calm rhythm as it moves across the land, gathering details and moments. Shaw's disappearance has implications throughout the novel, but it is never sensationalised or treated as the teleological focus. *Reservoir 13* signifies a contemporary shift away from the anthropocentric. This quality is noted by Ganteau: 'through narratorial impersonalisation, the human is humbled to the level of the animal, the vegetal and at times the mineral or elemental to build up a diffracted, kaleidoscopic landscape resonant with affect' (2018: section 9). By listing things without subordinating them, McGregor's paratactic prose situates human preoccupations next to the longer timescales of geology and climate. Both McGregor and French challenge the concepts of character and subjectivity in crime writing. Ashman, in his study on how ecological crime narratives respond to climate change, draws our attention to 'the value of reassessing the mode's traditions, conventions and forms for the ways they might yield new and enlightening perspectives on the entangled global histories of the Anthropocene' (2025: 2). McGregor and French offer their new perspectives by reconfiguring the genre tropes of loss and murder, enmeshing these anthropocentric concerns within novels that, via different methods, can be seen to foreground a host of alternative subjectivities, generated by and through the environment. The emphasis on place in crime series will be further intensified as authors respond to the current crisis and acknowledge that the most significant crime is what we humans are doing to the planet.

Another trend I predict, one that takes us from the environment into the heart of the home, is how the crime series adapts in response to the popularity of domestic-noir novels, such as Gillian Flynn's *Gone Girl* and Paula Hawkins's *The Girl on the Train*. Domestic noir is a relatively new addition to the crime genre, as an extension of the psychological thriller, and it continues to attract attention. Concerned with female experience, the novels typically feature violence and abuse in the context of family and relationships, often in a home environment and usually with a number of twists (Joyce & Sutton, 2018). Domestic-noir novels tend to be one-offs, with no sequels or prequels. However, among readers of crime fiction, there is a demand for recurring characters. Elsewhere in this study I have examined Liza Marklund's Annika Bengtzon series and shown how the author creates a feminised protagonist. In light of my earlier findings, I suggest that investigative journalist Bengtzon shares many of the traits of a domestic-noir character. Marklund's series offers a model for domestic-noir 'detective' series that will further challenge the genre's androcentric conventions (Latimer, 2021b).

Cosy crime is also expanding its boundaries, but Betz notes, 'Even though the cozy mystery has gained a wide audience, the works themselves receive very little critical attention' (2021: 2). In my study I have discussed examples of cosy crime, by Sujata Massey and Katherine Kovacic. It tends to be viewed as the least progressive category of the genre: 'the cozy appears to remove the complications that could result from including characters with the most discernible signifiers of otherness – race and sexuality' (Betz, 2021: 11). Writing against this trend, Massey dismantles otherness in her cosy crime series featuring a female lawyer, set in 1920s India: protagonist Perveen Mistry has Asian ethnicity; Mistry's closest friend, Alice Hobson-Jones, is queer. Cosy crime is associated with comforting entertainment rather than social critique, but Massey shows that the subgenre can embrace complex, often female-centred issues. In #1 *The Widows of Malabar Hill*, Mistry's experiences serve to highlight the restricted freedoms of Parsi women within their religion's matrimonial laws. In addition, there is a detailed account of the degradations caused by the orthodox practice of menstrual seclusion. The novel also addresses the Muslim tradition of women observing purdah, as well as their rights under Muslim inheritance laws. Alongside these concerns, the series interrogates the Raj and explores ideas of privilege: Mistry is subjected to prejudice from the white colonial rulers, but the protagonist recognises her own privilege as a wealthy, educated Indian in a continent with extremes of poverty and deprivation.

Massey skilfully negotiates these themes while retaining the qualities associated with cosy crime, such as a narrative centred on an amateur/semi-professional detective, with moments of humour, lightness of tone, descriptions of food and clothing, no profanities, no graphic descriptions of violence, and a limited death toll. Tripathi and Vijay point to the importance of Massey within the recent upsurge of Indian crime fiction written in English (2022: 142–3), a reminder that when evaluating a work, consideration needs to be given to regional factors. The protagonist Mistry is based on Cornelia Sorabji and Mithan Tata Lam, Indian women who pioneered the practice of law in India (143), and here again, Massey has extended the scope of cosy crime by showing that a series can draw inspiration from notable historical figures.

Innovations to cosy crime are also apparent in Katherine Kovacic's series featuring amateur detective Alex Clayton. The protagonist is an art dealer and central to the plot of #3 *The Shifting Landscape* is a painting of a homestead by Eugene von Guérard, 'one of the most significant artists in colonial Australia' (2020: 28). Von Guérard was a real person (1811–1901), and for the purposes of the novel Kovacic adds an undiscovered painting to his repertoire:

> On the very left of the frame, positioned so as not to obstruct the view of the homestead itself, are three Indigenous people – man, woman and child ... The woman gazes out of the painting, her eyes compelling the viewer's focus, but the man has turned to look over his shoulder, staring back at the land and the tiny white people tending the manicured gardens of Kinloch. Somehow von Guérard has created an incredibly powerful image of dispossession, while still managing to pander to his white settler patron's desire to showcase what they had achieved (28–9).

Kovacic is not Indigenous, but she uses her novel to challenge misrepresentations in art and fiction. As Turnbull notes, 'Despite the ways in which Kovacic might otherwise be described as writing "cosy" crime fiction, in the sense that the tone of her books is both light and playful, she is entirely serious in her treatment of Indigenous dispossession and the ways it has been conveyed in colonial art' (2023: 312–3). The theme is also explored through the character Harry, one of the Gunditjmara, the traditional owners of southwestern Victoria, who works at Kinloch on land stolen from his ancestors. Harry encourages Clayton to visit Budj Bim, a real location with the world's oldest aquaculture system where, for six thousand years, the Gunditjmara farmed eels and lived in stone huts (Kovacic, 2020: 113). He also tells Clayton about the massacre of his people by white settlers, Clayton reflecting, 'This is something every Australian should know' (114). Like Massey, Kovacic references real events, and both authors show that cosy crime is equipped to address complex themes such as prejudice, colonial rule, and Indigenous dispossession. This subgenre has been slow to embrace diversity and societal change, but the cosy crime series is on the verge of being reinvented, with authors like Massey and Kovacic leading the way.

New possibilities are also being generated by the continued growth in crossover fiction, where crime merges with other genres. Humann has written persuasively on 'hybridisation': 'contemporary crime writers – a much more diverse group than in past eras, not least due to the many female and non-white writers who are penning remarkable works of crime fiction – push the boundaries with respect to the genre, frequently transforming stories about crime and its consequences into hybrid or cross-genre works of fiction' (2020: 59). The hybridisation of crime fiction, Humann suggests, has allowed it to become 'a more suitable vehicle to call into question existing social norms, raise awareness about global issues and critique prevailing sociopolitical structures' (59). These topics and concerns have, to varying degrees, always been part of the genre, but the 'tools' an author uses to explore them are changing. At present, cross-genre crime novels tend to be one-offs, for instance Riley Sager's *Home Before Dark*, with its 'supernatural elements playing into a classic murder mystery' (Fracassi, 2023). Another is Sarah Pinborough's *Mayhem*, a standalone crime novel that combines police procedural with the horror genre. For those seeking cross-genre experimentation in series form, such as Paul Johnston's near-future dystopian Quint Dalrymple series, the place to look is the smaller publishing houses.

The shift toward hybrid/cross-genre crime series is, at present, more apparent in TV, for example, Steven Conrad's drama *Patriot* (2015–18). Premiered on Amazon, it is a mix of dark comedy, spy thriller, political drama, and police procedural. Set in 2012, CIA operative John Tavner, played by John Dorman, goes undercover as an industrial engineer at a US company. Via a trade delegation to Luxembourg, Tavner will secretly deliver funds to secure the success of the moderate candidate in the upcoming election in Iran, thereby preventing the country from developing nuclear arms. If Tavner fails, the outcome could be world war. The plot summary reflects the tropes in spy thrillers, but Conrad dismantles and reassembles these familiar parts into something new, unsettling, and nihilistic, that constantly shifts from comedy to tragedy.

The aspect I wish to highlight in *Patriot* is the hero's journey. As Season 1 opens, Tavner is on sick leave, as a career of killing has damaged his mental health. Groomed to be an assassin by his father, a senior figure in the CIA, Tavner now dreams of being a folk singer, but his father needs him to complete one last mission. The episodes chart the protagonist's decline, mentally and physically, alongside his transformation from lone hero, isolated and self-reliant, to embedded hero, surrounded and supported by a growing list of helpers (his brother, wife, mother, and colleagues from the engineering firm) and the mission becomes saving Tavner as well as saving the world. Across two seasons and eighteen episodes, *Patriot* documents the feminising of a mythorealist protagonist who has been traumatised by masculinity. And it is by borrowing from different genres, such as dark comedy and the police procedural, that Conrad is able to create this original and thought-provoking drama. Other notable examples of hybrid TV series that have experimented with genre are HBO's crime drama *The Sopranos* (1999–2007), Showtime's crime drama *Dexter* (2006–2013), and BBC America/BBC Three's spy thriller *Killing Eve* (2018–2022).

True crime is also exerting a growing influence on our notions of a crime series. There are numerous true-crime podcasts that effectively function as crime series, with the narrator solving (or at least attempting to solve) a new case each season while also frequently offering listeners a glimpse into the narrator's personal life. These podcasts are in turn inspiring hybrid works of crime fiction, for example, Matt Wesolowski's *Hydra* and Denise Mina's *Conviction*, both of which feature a (fictional) true-crime podcast. Disney's mystery comedy *Only Murders in the Building* (2021–) is another indicator of the prevalence of true-crime podcasts within contemporary culture. The podcast is reconfiguring crime narratives in fiction and drama, and it is likely to inspire future innovations in the series form.

These days, audiences and readerships are well-versed in the many genres that shape our culture, due to increased availability and exposure to a range of media: film, TV, novels, audiobooks, and podcasts. On a streaming service such as Amazon or Netflix, the interface has recommendations relating to previous selections; this invites a viewer to navigate in different directions and make discoveries. In the traditional publishing sector, crime fiction series still seem confined to a restricted set of subgenres (police procedural, thriller, and cosy), perhaps because of the perceived difficulties of marketing works that either stray too far from the familiar or are split across two distinct genres (e.g., crime and sci-fi). Conrad's *Patriot* was made for TV, but if the medium had been a series of novels it is questionable whether the content would have attracted a mainstream publisher.

There is risk attached to a crime fiction series, as it often entails the publisher initially commissioning two or three novels. Many series fail to retain a readership, and an author will be encouraged to launch a new series with an alternative protagonist. Already established in the marketplace are big-name authors including Lee Child, Michael Connelly, Patricia Cornwell, Janet Evanovich, Marcia Muller, Ian Rankin, and Karin Slaughter, whose series grow to 15, 20, and 25+ novels, but when considered within the crime genre as a whole, such duration and commercial successes have been rare. The situation is, however, changing. Many series authors choose to self-publish, and platforms like Kindle Direct Publishing are transforming the range and number of crime series available to readers.

The traditional boundaries around crime fiction will become increasingly fluid, reflecting the evolving tastes that are the inevitable outcome of new generations of readers. In addition, the genre is adapting to internationalisation, with crime series widely distributed through editions in translation, leading to influences from across the globe. All these emerging trends can be facilitated by the development of online tools for marketing crime fiction in more sophisticated ways: readers will be introduced to series from other countries, and they will also discover additional less familiar subgenres and hybrid/cross-genre works that subvert existing categories.

In an increasingly digital-savvy world, especially among a younger readership, the interface with readers will become more like the interface currently seen on streaming services such as Netflix. Another growth area is BookTok, a subcommunity on the TikTok app, and although at present it tends to focus on young adult fiction, this is likely to change as the participants age, and publishers make more use of BookTok to promote crime series. These different ways of engaging with literature, accessible through a phone rather than via a bookshop, will encourage and enable hybridisation. Reflecting the viewing and reading tastes of the younger generation, I foresee an upsurge in three areas: series that merge crime with horror/supernatural fiction; series that merge crime with fantasy fiction; and series that merge crime with romantic fiction.

Looking ahead to the ways in which the crime genre will continue to diversify and hybridise, one firm conclusion is apparent: the drive to feminise the mythorealist figure of the protagonist, a trend that developed in the crime fiction series, has become the dominant requirement in all crime series of the 2020s, in whichever format, fiction or TV or film. Readers and viewers want a relatable detective figure who is obsessively pursuing the murder quest at the same time as coping with personal dilemmas. They want someone with a backstory, who is overcoming formative incidents from childhood. They want a protagonist who is navigating complex relationships with a spouse/partner, family, friends, colleagues, and the wider community.

When the murder is solved, when the novel is put away or the TV switched off, when the intricacies of the plot are forgotten, the person we remember is the protagonist. Crime is no longer the main focus. Instead, the contemporary crime series has become a long and detailed enquiry into the human condition. These detective figures have a gravitational pull, a life-affirming longevity, they endure against the bounds of reason, and against the odds of fictional possibility. They offer us ways of exploring who we are, why we are here on this planet, who we love, what we value, and who we are frightened of losing. And by keeping on striving, page after page, book after book, year after year, these characters show us that it takes a lifetime to answer the questions that really matter.

7 Writing a Crime Fiction Series

This Element celebrates crime series as works of literature that are sophisticated, complex, and beautifully crafted. However, by revealing the conventions there is the risk of reinforcing the stereotype that crime series are rule-based and rigidly formulaic, a view completely at odds with my own position. Therefore I offer some important caveats along with this guide to writing a series. The genre has always embraced huge variation and its conventions facilitate creativity rather than restricting it. I am a crime fiction researcher and teacher, but I am also an author of detective fiction. My desire to share with other creative writers this deliberately playful guide is to enrich your understanding of the inner workings of the genre and, I hope, provide a source of inspiration, an impetus to experiment and subvert and innovate. I am not issuing rules or proscriptions. The following is a record of the many years I have spent reading, writing, studying, and loving crime series.

The opening gambits

Who is your lead character/detective?

How is the story being told: first-person 'I', second-person 'you', third-person 'she/he/they', maybe a combination?

Written in present tense, past tense, or with elements of both?

Who is dead/about to die?

Who is the killer?

Where and when is it set?

Which subgenre: thriller, neo-hardboiled, cosy crime, etc., or cross-genre/hybridised?

Who's in charge?

There are three main types of protagonist:

Professional detective who is in police service or a private investigator, and is employed to solve a murder.

Semi-professional detective who solves a murder using transferrable skills from their role as a lawyer, forensic pathologist, forensic psychologist, investigative journalist, and other comparable occupations.

Amateur detective, also known as amateur sleuth, who stumbles on a murder and feels compelled to solve it, often for personal reasons; they have a day job unrelated to crime, such as chef, jockey, archaeologist, florist, librarian, artist, and so on.

The figure you devise might be hybrid, merging different aspects from these three categories.

How many detectives?

A crime series tends to have at its centre the detective figure.

The detective could be solo or part of a duo (e.g., a series featuring a police detective and a journalist).

There could be a third protagonist, bringing an alternative perspective to the narrative (e.g., a friend of the murder victim).

An author is free to explore multiple and varied protagonists, but it is worth bearing in mind that readers enjoy bonding with the lead characters, and this is more challenging if there are lots of protagonists vying for the reader's loyalties.

How do I know it's them?

The protagonist has a set of identifying traits, such as physical appearance, gender, sexuality, ethnicity, nationality, age, job, behaviour patterns, belief system, and personality.

Traits tend to remain fairly consistent in a series, so reader recognises it is the same person in each novel.

Traits are conveyed via description and via protagonist's actions, dialogue with different characters, and inner monologue, where protagonist is shown thinking about themselves or others and the world around them.

In a series there may be vignettes/small scenes that repeat (with different wording) in each book, and which frame the protagonist in a particular setting that reflects their key traits; these vignettes are associated with habitual things the protagonist does and usually emerge as an organic part of how you portray them.

If the overall timeframe for a series is spread across a number of (fictional) years, then protagonist is likely to mature, physically and mentally.

These changes tend to be limited, and protagonist rarely undergoes any drastic transformation; this rather 'static' convention could easily be challenged, and new authors may create characters that change more radically across the series arc.

How is the story being told?

First-person point of view (I am the detective telling you the story): protagonist is sole narrator of the investigation that unfolds; reader can only know what protagonist knows about the case.

Series written in first-person can (if author chooses) include other passages narrated by a witness, killer, victim, and so on, meaning the reader can learn things the detective does not know.

If the additional voices are first-person, it could leave the reader wondering 'whose head am I in, the detective or somebody else?'; to avoid confusion, a possible approach is to narrate additional voices in third-person.

Third-person point of view (she/he is the detective telling you the story; they [non-binary] are the detective telling you the story): it could be third-person subjective/'close third', where detective's thoughts/feelings are shared with the reader, and thus it is similar to first-person point of view; or it could be third-person objective, where the reader is more distanced from detective's thoughts/feelings.

Series written in third-person can (if author chooses) include additional passages narrated by other characters.

Typical plot

A series novel usually starts with a murder or crime in the opening chapter(s).

Reader is kept in the moment, following the investigation, gathering clues along with the detective figure.

Novel ends when murderer is apprehended or killed (trial/court scenes assumed to happen afterwards).

Next novel begins when protagonist starts a new investigation about a different crime.

Protagonist pursues the murder quest, but the novel also includes events in their personal life; these personal events create an ongoing biography for protagonist, who has a 'life' that persists between novels.

At the end of each novel the murder story is concluded when protagonist apprehends the killer; protagonist's life story continues and is the strand that joins the series together.

More about plot

Protagonist is pursing different lines of enquiry.

There may be several suspects and the reader is kept guessing about the killer.

Protagonist gathers clues, determining if they are: false clues, which prove to be red herrings/misdirections; true clues, which lead to discoveries that unravel the mystery.

Protagonist meets obstacles to their enquiries, along with peril/danger, and often their own life is at risk.

Protagonist navigates toward a fuller understanding, via a sequence of breakthroughs and revelations.

Example of a plot: protagonist is investigating two unrelated cases that turn out to be linked; halfway through the novel, protagonist speculates that both cases are connected; this means the reader feels part of the investigation and not completely in the dark; it also means the threads start weaving together, but to create an impact in the finale it always helps to keep a few twists and surprises until the very end.

Forgive and forget

Protagonist is focused on the current murder and tends to 'forget' previous novels in the series.

Protagonist rarely recalls details of those earlier investigations or the trauma they went through.

Identity of murderer in previous novels is usually not revealed in later ones (the series might not be read in chronological order, hence the tendency to avoid 'spoilers').

Reader invests their emotions and attention in current novel, and lengthy explanations about previous ones could be distracting and slow the pace.

However, there are series with lots of continuity between instalments and the author is writing in the expectation that the books will be read in chronological order.

The degree of continuity, and the incorporation or exclusion of references to previous books, is down to the author and the type of series you are creating.

Masculinised protagonist – no baggage

Protagonist has few personal commitments and a limited home life.

Protagonist is: single, maybe in an on-off relationship, or divorced/separated; childless or semi-estranged from their children, though they may have a niece/nephew they see occasionally.

Protagonist is often an 'orphan', meaning no ageing parent requiring support.

Protagonist is usually a loner, and any friendships will tend to be with someone in law enforcement.

Lack of personal commitments means protagonist is free to focus on murder quest, without distractions.

These conventions produce a masculinised protagonist; their personal life provides background texture rather than being a central concern.

Masculinised protagonist can be female, male, trans, non-binary; 'masculinised' refers to behaviour not anatomy.

Feminised protagonist – excess luggage

Protagonist has lots of personal commitments and a fully developed home life (not necessarily a 'nuclear family', but likely to feature some of these: spouse/partner, children, relatives, friends, colleagues, local community).

Protagonist conducts an investigation at same time as fulfilling personal/domestic commitments, including caring for relatives/friends; coping with these conflicting demands is often challenging for the protagonist.

These conventions tend to produce a feminised protagonist; their personal life is a central concern, but the murder quest remains a priority.

Feminised protagonist can be female, male, trans, non-binary; 'feminised' refers to behaviour not anatomy.

Myth or mortal?

Masculinised protagonist resembles a mythic hero: superior mental and/or physical abilities; focused on a quest that entails overcoming challenges; invincible/immortal, rarely ageing much.

Masculinised protagonist also resembles a regular human being: they have an ongoing biography that follows a chronological arc; they have feelings and worries; they make mistakes; their personal life goes through ups and downs that are unpredictable.

Masculinised protagonist combines myth with reality and is a 'mythorealist' character.

Feminised protagonist is also mythorealist, but they have a more developed personal life and seem more 'real'.

Crime series protagonists can be placed on a spectrum from masculinised and more obviously mythic, to feminised and more obviously realist.

Murder is the name of the game

Regardless of the type of protagonist (masculinised or feminised), the murder quest is their priority and most of the novel is devoted to their active on-duty mode.

Occupying a smaller proportion is the protagonist in off-duty mode, during the non-working hours that feature their personal life.

We all have complicated lives, with pressures, demands, disagreements; the same is true of protagonist.

Scenes about personal life can vary the rhythms in a crime novel and modulate (but not deplete) the tension.

In series with a feminised protagonist there is more personal life, but it is usually confined to about a quarter/third of the novel and the majority tends to be about the murder quest.

Reader only gets to read about protagonist's personal life when they have a murder to solve.

These are crime series, and if protagonist goes on holiday, the chances are someone will die.

Timeframe

Each series novel typically happens in a tight timeframe, from a few days up to a few weeks.

Pace matters in a crime novel, and a way of instilling pace is to compress the events into fewer days.

However, this is up to the author; a longer timeframe can still generate pace, depending how it is written.

In limbo

Everything goes quiet in the gaps between each novel of a crime series.

Protagonist only appears on the page when a murder happens, and after the murder is solved, they return to being in limbo.

A slightly open ending is a feature of contemporary crime series; the protagonist's 'job' is over once the murder is solved, but reader may be left with questions about protagonist's personal life, and reader also likes a hint that protagonist will reappear in a future investigation.

Backstory

Protagonist has a past, consisting of a childhood and formative events from their younger years.

When protagonist recalls moments from their backstory, it makes them seem like a real person.

Reading a series can be a process of discovery, learning new details about protagonist and their backstory.

A possible approach is to spread aspects of this backstory across different instalments, rather than reveal everything in book one.

Engagement

People read series because they form a bond with the main character.

The murder plot has significance during those hours when the reader is reading the novel.

Once the novel ends, what the reader tends to retain is that connection to the protagonist and the world they inhabit.

This is why it is important to create a complex and engaging and intriguing detective figure, somebody the reader (and author) wants to spend time with, book after book after book.

Emotional arc

What are the protagonist's motivations: identifying the killer, but what else?

Personal issues they are struggling to resolve?

An event in their past that hangs over them?

Pay attention to the emotional arc of your detective figure.

If the story is overly focused on cliffhangers, fights and chase scenes, the reader may lose interest.

Too much action becomes relentless and boring if there is not enough about emotional arc of protagonist.

On the other hand, introspection and musing about existence can slow the pace; but omit this altogether, and reader might struggle to bond with protagonist.

In most series there is a mix of action and introspection, to varying degrees.

Secondary characters are people too

Series always contain a host of secondary characters:

– one-off characters who only appear in a single book.

– recurring characters, such as family and friends of protagonist, or work colleagues.

An author pays close attention to creating the detective figure, making them complicated, layered, realistic.

Secondary characters also deserve to be nurtured.

Who's to blame?

Regardless of the subgenre or type of detective figure, most contemporary series explore a set of themes, often directed at society and the causes of crime.

The murderer is to blame, but so is society, because crime is rooted in societal problems.

An additional method for exploring such themes is through a feminised protagonist, where events in the detective figure's personal life are mirrored with events in the murder quest, thereby emphasising the inequalities and negative influences that afflict home lives as well as wider society.

Authority figures?

Masculinised protagonist typically has status and privilege within society (e.g., because of gender or race) and their authority as 'the detective' is rarely challenged.

Feminised protagonist typically belongs to a disadvantaged group that lacks privilege in society (e.g., because of gender or race) and their authority as 'the detective' is frequently challenged; expressing these challenges in the novels then becomes a further way of drawing attention to structural inequalities.

Old habits are hard to break

Ever since the 1840s, most crime fiction series have featured a masculinised protagonist.

This was modified in 1970s by feminist authors writing female detective figures, but even nowadays these tend to reflect masculine norms.

The only character type to challenge this is the feminised protagonist; they started appearing in the 1990s but are still relatively uncommon.

The crime genre accommodates many variations on the detective figure, masculinised, feminised, or somewhere in between, and each author is free to experiment.

Setting

A crime series creates a fictional world and the reader enters that world on opening each book.

A crime series is often rooted in a particular city or region, but others explore larger territories.

Detective figure is frequently on the move, examining crime scenes, gathering clues, visiting witnesses, chasing suspects, or being pursued by the killer, and therefore setting is a major component.

Foreground not background

Setting becomes a living character, which changes and develops from book to book.

Setting is somewhere the reader can visualise and engage with using all their senses.

Setting can convey the psychological mood of the book and why a violent crime has occurred.

Descriptions of setting help reader understand the socioeconomics and politics of a particular era and place.

Setting also communicates the subgenre: the chase scenes in a thriller, full of tension; the lush descriptions in cosy crime, with references to food and clothing; the brooding menace of noir interiors.

Worth spending time on choosing where to set your series, a place that intrigues you and which you enjoy exploring through words.

The rule is . . . there are no rules

This how-to guide is about possibilities not prohibitions.

My definitions are broad and flexible, and can be considered, subverted, challenged.

My aim is to increase our understanding of crime series and inspire creativity.

Remember this

Crimes series are about people not crimes.

And the most significant person is the detective.

Who are they?

What drives them?

Even when surrounded by family and friends, the detective feels isolated.

Obsessed with the murder quest, the detective sacrifices everyone and everything for the sake of answers.

But those answers never satisfy, and the detective is always looking for the next killing, the next investigation.

Strip away gender, and what you are left with is a perpetual outcast on a perpetual mission.

Resolution and absolution will always be out of reach.

No respite ever

This applies to the author, the detective, the reader.

Once a crime series has a grip on you, it never lets go.

References

Abbott, Megan E. (2002). *The Street Was Mine: White Masculinity and Urban Space in Hardboiled Fiction and Film Noir*, New York: Palgrave Macmillan.

Anderson, Jean, Miranda, Carolina, & Pezzotti, Barbara (2015). Introduction. In Anderson, Miranda and Pezzotti, editors, *Serial Crime Fiction: Dying for More*. Basingstoke: Palgrave Macmillan, pp. 1–7.

Ashman, Nathan (2025). *Crime Fiction and Ecology: From the Local to the Global*, Cambridge: Cambridge University Press.

Bergman, Kerstin (2014). *Swedish Crime Fiction: The Making of Nordic Noir*, Milan: Mimesis International.

Bergman, Kerstin (2015). From Conflicted Mother to Lone Avenger: Transformations of the Woman Journalist Detective in Liza Marklund's Crime Series. In Jean Anderson, Carolina Miranda and Barbara Pezzotti, editors, *Serial Crime Fiction: Dying for More*. Basingstoke: Palgrave Macmillan, pp. 111–21.

Betz, Phyllis M. (2021). Introduction. In Phyllis M. Betz, editor, *Reading the Cozy Mystery: Essays on an Underappreciated Genre*. Jefferson: McFarland, pp. 1–16.

Caldwell, Nicholas & Harris, Steven (2024). A Transfiguration Paradigm for Quest Design. *Games and Culture Sage Journals*, 19(4), 493–512. journals.sagepub.com/doi/full/10.1177/15554120231170152.

Campbell, Joseph (1973). *The Hero with a Thousand Faces*, Princeton: Princeton University Press.

Campbell, Joseph & Moyers, Bill (1991). *The Power of Myth*, New York: Anchor.

Chambers, William & Chambers, Robert (1843). The London Police. In William Chambers and Robert Chambers, editors, *Chambers's Edinburgh Journal*. Edinburgh: W. & R. Chambers, 12(7), 54.

Child, Lee (2007). *Bad Luck and Trouble* (#11), London: Bantam.

Child, Lee (2010a). *Killing Floor* (#1), London: Bantam.

Child, Lee (2010b). *61 Hours* (#14), London: Bantam.

Child, Lee (2012). *The Affair* (#16), London: Bantam.

Child, Lee (2013). *Never Go Back* (#18), London: Bantam.

Child, Lee (2018). Interviewed by Elspeth Latimer. 20 July, Harrogate.

Coupe, Laurence (2010). Foreword. In Amina Alyal and Paul Hardwick, editors, *Classical and Contemporary Mythic Identities: Construction of the Literary Imagination*. Lewiston: Mellen Press, pp. xi–xiii.

Creeber, Glen (2004). *Serial Television*, London: B.F.I.

Danielsson, Karin Molander (2002). *The Dynamic Detective: Special Interest and Seriality in Contemporary Detective Series*, Uppsala: Uppsala University.

Danielsson, Karin Molander (2003). The Private Life of the Series Detective. In Eva Lambertsson Björk, Karen Patrick Knutsen, and Elin Nesje Vestli, editors, *Modi Operandi: Perspektiver på Kriminanllitteratur*. Halden: Østfold University College. ia.hiof.no/~borres/krim/pdffiler/Danielsson.pdf.

Danyté, Milda (2011). *Introduction to the Analysis of Crime Fiction: A User-friendly Guide*, Kaunas: Vytautas Magnus University.

Durot-Boucé, Elizabeth (2004). 'Chew You Up and Spit You Out': Rewriting a Familiar Fixture of the Gothic Novel. *Anglophonia*, 15, 209–16.

Eco, Umberto (2005). The Myth of Superman. In Jeet Heer and Kent Worcester, editors, *Arguing Comics: Literary Masters on a Popular Medium*. Jackson: Mississippi University, pp. 146–64. (Originally published in 1962 as 'El mito di Superman e la dissoluzione del tempo'.)

Felski, Rita (2015). Latour and Literary Studies. *PMLA*, 130(3), 737–742.

Fracassi, Philip (2023). Crossing the Streams: Novels That Will Chill and Thrill! *CrimeReads*, 12 July. crimereads.com/crossing-the-streams-novels-that-will-thrill-and-chill/.

Frankel, Valerie Estelle (2010). *From Girl to Goddess: The Heroine's Journey through Myth and Legend*, Jefferson: McFarland.

French, Tana (2013). *Broken Harbour* (#4), London: Hodder & Stoughton.

Gadamer, Hans-Georg (2000). Subjectivity and Intersubjectivity, Subject and Person. *Continental Philosophy Review*, 33(3), 275–87.

Ganteau Jean-Michel (2018). Diffracted Landscapes of Attention: Jon McGregor's *Reservoir 13*. *Études britanniques contemporaines*, 55, sections 1–22.

Heidbrink, Henriette (2010). Fictional Characters in Literary and Media Studies: A Survey of the Research. In Jens Eder, Fotis Jannidis, and Ralf Schneider, editors, *Characters in Fictional Worlds: Understanding Imaginary Beings in Literature, Film, and Other Media*. Berlin: de Gruyter, pp. 67–110.

Hill, Lorna (2017). *Bloody Women: A Critical-Creative Examination of How Female Protagonists Have Transformed Contemporary Scottish and Nordic Crime Fiction*. Ph.D. Thesis. Stirling University.

Hudson, Kim (2010). *The Virgin's Promise: Writing Stories of Feminine Creative, Spiritual, and Sexual Awakening*, Los Angeles: Michael Wiese Productions.

Humann, Heather Duerre (2020). Hybridisation. In Janice Allan, Jesper Gulddal, Stewart King and Andrew Pepper, editors, *The Routledge Companion to Crime Fiction*. London: Routledge, pp. 57–64.

Jameson, Fredric (2016). *Raymond Chandler: The Detections of Totality*, New York: Verso.

Jones, Manina & Walton, Priscilla L. (1999). *Detective Agency: Women Rewriting the Hard-Boiled Tradition*, Berkeley: California University.

Joyce, Laura & Sutton, Henry, editors (2018). *Domestic Noir: The New Face of 21st Century Crime Fiction*, Cham: Palgrave Macmillan.

Keane, Niall & Lawn, Chris (2011). *The Gadamer Dictionary*, London: Continuum International.

Kinsman, Margaret (2002). A Band of Sisters. In Warren Chernaik, Martin Swales and Robert Vilain, editors, *The Art of Detective Fiction*. Basingstoke: Palgrave Macmillan, pp. 153–69.

Kovacic, Katherine (2019). *Painting in the Shadows* (#2), Kindle edition by Echo Publishing (location indicators with respect to 3784 locations for whole eBook).

Kovacic, Katherine (2020). *The Shifting Landscape* (#3), London: Echo.

Latimer, Elspeth (2020). *Character Poetics in the Contemporary Crime Fiction Series*. Ph.D. Thesis. University of East Anglia.

Latimer, Elspeth (2021a). Place as a Character in the Contemporary Crime Fiction Series. In Charlotte Beyer, editor, *Contemporary Crime Fiction: Crossing Boundaries, Merging Genres*. Newcastle upon Tyne: Cambridge Scholars, pp. 158–186.

Latimer, Elspeth (2021b). Home and Home-less: Narrating and Negating the Domestic in Contemporary Crime Fiction Series. *Clues, A Journal of Detection*, 39(1), 72–85.

Levay, Matthew (2019). *Violent Minds*, Cambridge: Cambridge University Press.

Locke, Attica (2018). *Bluebird, Bluebird* (#1), London: Serpent's Tail.

Malmgren, Carl (2010). The Pursuit of Crime: Characters in Crime Fiction. In Charles J. Rzepka and Lee Horsley, editors, *A Companion to Crime Fiction*. Chichester: Wiley-Blackwell, pp. 152–63.

Margolin, Uri (2007). Character. In David Herman, editor, *The Cambridge Companion to Narrative*. Cambridge: Cambridge University Press, pp. 66–79.

Marklund, Liza (2011a). Liza Marklund: Exposed. Interviewed by Vanessa Fox O'Loughlin. *Writing.ie*. 10 August. writing.ie/special-guests/liza-marklund-exposed/.

References

Marklund, Liza (2011b). *The Bomber* (Chronological Order #4), Translated by Neil Smith, London: Corgi.

Marklund, Liza (2012). *Last Will* (Chronological Order #6), Translated by Neil Smith, London: Corgi.

Massey, Sujata (2018). *The Widows of Malabar Hill* (#1), New York: Soho Press.

Massey, Sujata (2023). *The Mistress of Bhatia House* (#4), New York: Soho Press.

Mayer, Ruth (2020). The Crime Fiction Series. In Janice Allan, Jesper Gulddal, Stewart King and Andrew Pepper, editors, *The Routledge Companion to Crime Fiction*. London: Routledge, pp. 31–38.

McGregor, Jon (2018). *Reservoir 13*, London: 4th Estate.

Miller, David A. (1988). *The Novel and the Police*, Berkeley: California University.

Mina, Denise (2007). Murder She Wrote – and Plenty of It: Denise Mina on Her Career. Interviewed by Peter Guttridge. *The Observer*, 29 July. theguardian.com/books/2007/jul/29/crimebooks.features.

Mosley, Walter (2005). *Little Scarlet* (#9), London: Phoenix.

Mosley, Walter (2014). *Little Green* (#12), London: Phoenix.

Mosley, Walter (2015). *Rose Gold* (#13), London: Weidenfeld & Nicolson.

Most, Glenn W. (1983). The Hippocratic Smile: John le Carré and the Traditions of the Detective Novel. In Glenn W. Most and William W. Stowe, editors, *The Poetics of Murder: Detective Fiction and Literary Theory*. San Diego: Harcourt Brace Jovanovich, pp. 341–65.

Munt, Sally R. (2004). *Murder by the book? Feminism and the Crime novel*, eBook (first published 1995), London: Routledge.

Neely, Barbara (2020). *All Four Novels* (#1 *Blanche on the Lam*; #2 *Blanche among the Talented Tenth*; #3 *Blanche Cleans Up*; #4 *Blanche Passes Go*), Kindle edition by Brash Books (location indicators with respect to 15879 locations for whole eBook).

Plain, Gill (2001). *Twentieth Century Crime Fiction: Gender, Sexuality and the Body*. Edinburgh: Edinburgh University.

Plain, Gill (2002). *Ian Rankin's* Black and Blue: *A Reader's Guide*, London: Continuum International.

Rabinowitz, Peter (2002). 'I Never Saw Any of Them Again': Series, Sequels, and Character Identity. Paper (unpublished) Given at International Conference on Narrative, Michigan State University. Cited by Richardson (2010) in Transtextual Characters. Upon request, Rabinowitz emailed a copy on 10 January 2017.

Rankin, Ian (2001). *Resurrection Men* (#13), London: Orion.

Rankin, Ian (2003). *Let It Bleed* (#7 pp. 1–228) in *Rebus: The Lost Years*, London: Orion.
Rankin, Ian (2006). *Rebus's Scotland: A Personal Journey*, London: Orion.
Rankin, Ian (2008). *Exit Music* (#17), London: Orion.
Rankin, Ian (2011a). *Knots and Crosses* (#1), London: Orion.
Rankin, Ian (2011b). *Hide and Seek* (#2), London: Orion.
Rankin, Ian (2011c). *The Black Book* (#5), London: Orion.
Rankin, Ian (2012). Interview with Ian Rankin by Stefani Sloma on 14 June, 2011, Edinburgh. Appendix 1 of The City as Character: Edinburgh in the Works of Ian Rankin. *The Researcher: An Interdisciplinary Journal*. Jackson: Jackson State University, 25(2), 71–91.
Rankin, Ian (2016). Interviewed by Elspeth Latimer. 1 December, Norwich.
Rankin, Ian (2019). *In a House of Lies* (#22), London: Orion.
Richardson, Brian (2010). Transtextual Characters. In Jens Eder, Fotis Jannidis and Ralf Schneider, editors, *Characters in Fictional Worlds: Understanding Imaginary Beings in Literature, Film, and Other Media*. Berlin: de Gruyter, pp. 527–41.
Rosen, Jeremy (2016). *Minor Characters Have Their Day: Genre and the Contemporary Literary Marketplace*, New York: Columbia University.
Sloma, Stefani (2012). The City as Character: Edinburgh in the Works of Ian Rankin. *The Researcher: An Interdisciplinary Journal*. Jackson: Jackson State University, 25(2), 53–95.
Soitos, Stephen F. (1996). *The Blues Detective: a Study of African American Detective Fiction*, Amherst: Massachusetts University.
Spindler, Robert (2013). German Saddle Pals and the Absence of Love in the Karl May Westerns. In Sue Matheson, editor, *Love in Western Film and Television: Lonely Hearts and Happy Trails*. New York: Palgrave Macmillan, pp. 209–24.
Stoddard Holmes, Martha (1997). Between Men: How Ruth Rendell Reads for Gender. In Jerome H. Delamater and Ruth Prigozy, editors, *Theory and Practice of Classic Detective Fiction*. Westport: Greenwood Press, pp. 149–58.
Strong, Jeremy (2020). Character Adaptations: Recurrence and Return. *Adaptation*, 14(1), 109–35.
Sutton, Henry (2023). *Crafting Crime Fiction*, Manchester: Manchester University.
Tripathi, Priyanka & Vijay, Febin (2022). Appropriating a Hostile Genre: Feminist Concerns in Contemporary Indian Women's Crime Fiction. *IUP Journal of English Studies*, 17(2), 140–55.

Turnbull, Sue (2023). Monstrous Wounds: Crime, Environmental Catastrophe and Domestic Abuse in Jane Harper's *The Dry*. *Journal of Australian Studies*, 47(2), 309–21.

Vanacker, Sabine (2011). 'A Visitor for the Dead': Adam Dalgliesh as a Serial Detective. In Malcah Effron, editor, *The Millennial Detective: Essays on Trends in Crime Fiction, Film and Television, 1990–2010*. Jefferson: McFarland, pp. 66–81.

Vanacker, Sabine (2015). Series Fiction and the Challenge of Ideology: The Feminism of Sara Paretsky. In Jean Anderson, Carolina Miranda and Barbara Pezzotti, editors, *Serial Crime Fiction: Dying for More*. Basingstoke: Palgrave Macmillan, pp. 99–110.

Acknowledgements

An earlier version of parts of this study appeared in my Ph.D. thesis (2020): I would like to thank my doctoral supervisors Henry Sutton and Clare Connors for all their insights, encouragement, and support; and I am grateful to CHASE, the Consortium for the Humanities and the Arts South-East England, for funding my Ph.D.

I would also like to express my gratitude to C.U.P. Series Editors Margot Douaihy, Catherine Nickerson, and Henry Sutton, for their detailed advice and guidance on my Element.

Finally, I wish to thank my two (anonymous) peer reviewers for their insights and suggestions.

Permissions

Extracts from my interview with Lee Child are published with his kind permission.

Extracts from my interview with Ian Rankin are published with his kind permission.

Extracts from Sujata Massey's novels are reproduced with kind permission of Soho Press.

About the Author

Elspeth Latimer has a Ph.D. in crime series from the University of East Anglia, where she is associate tutor in crime writing. She was awarded a UEA Visiting Fellowship to research the Lee Child Archive. Shortlisted for the Bath Novel Award, her crime novel *The Lost Detective* is published by Story Machine.

Cambridge Elements

Crime Narratives

Margot Douaihy
Emerson College

Margot Douaihy, PhD, is an assistant professor at Emerson College in Boston. She is the author of *Scorched Grace* (Gillian Flynn Books/Zando, 2023), which was named one of the best crime novels of 2023 by *The New York Times*, *The Guardian*, and *CrimeReads*. Her recent scholarship includes 'Beat the Clock: Queer Temporality and Disrupting Chrononormativity in Crime Fiction', a NeMLA 2024 paper.

Catherine Nickerson
Emory College of Arts and Sciences

Catherine Ross Nickerson is the author of *The Web of Iniquity: Early Detective Fiction by American Women* (Duke University Press, 1999), which was nominated for an Edgar Award by the Mystery Writers of America. She is the editor of *The Cambridge Companion to American Crime Fiction* (2010), as well as two volumes of reprinted novels by Anna Katharine Green and Metta Fuller Victor (Duke University Press).

Henry Sutton
University of East Anglia

Henry Sutton, SFHEA, is Professor of Creative Writing and Crime Fiction at the University of East Anglia. He is the author of fifteen novels, including two crime fiction series. He is also the author of *Crafting Crime Fiction* (Manchester University Press, 2023), and the co-editor of *Domestic Noir: The New Face of 21st Century Crime Fiction* (Palgrave Macmillan, 2018).

Advisory Board

William Black, *Johns Hopkins University*
Christopher Breu, *Illinois State University*
Cathy Cole, *Liverpool John Moores University and University of Wollongong*
Stacy Gillis, *Newcastle University*
Femi Kayode, *Author (Namibia)*
Richie Narvaez, *Fashion Institute of Technology*
Andrew Pepper, *Belfast University*
Barbara Pezzotti, *Monash University*
Clare Rolens, *Palomar College*
Shampa Roy, *University of Delhi*
David Schmid, *University of Buffalo*
Samantha Walton, *Bath Spa University*
Aliki Varvogli, *University of Dundee*

About the Series

Publishing groundbreaking research from scholars and practitioners of crime writing in its many dynamic and evolving forms, this series examines and re-examines crime narratives as a global genre which began on the premise of entertainment, but quickly evolved to probe pressing political and sociological concerns, along with the human condition.

Cambridge Elements

Crime Narratives

Elements in the Series

Forensic Crime Fiction
Aliki Varvogli

Female Anger in Crime Fiction
Caroline Reitz

Crime Fiction and Ecology: From the Local to the Global
Nathan Ashman

Bloodlines: Adoption, Crime, and the Search for Belonging
Jinny Huh

Writing the Detectives: Character and the Series Form
Elspeth Latimer

A full series listing is available at: www.cambridge.org/ECNA

For EU product safety concerns, contact us at Calle de José Abascal, 56–1°,
28003 Madrid, Spain or eugpsr@cambridge.org.